GOOD INDIAN GIRLS

Ranbir Singh Sidhu was born in London and grew up in California. He is a playwright and a winner of the Pushcart Prize in fiction, among other awards. Trained as an archaeologist specializing in human and animal bone studies, he has worked throughout the western United States, Israel and France. He currently lives in New York.

GOOD INDIAN GIRLS

Stories

Ranbir Singh Sidhu

HarperCollins *Publishers* India

First published in India by
HarperCollins *Publishers* in 2012

Building No 10, Tower A, 4th Floor, DLF Cyber City, Phase II,
Gurugram – 122002
www.harpercollins.co.in

2 4 6 8 10 9 7 5 3

P-ISBN: 978-93-5029-396-6
E-ISBN: 978-93-5029-925-8

Typeset in 12/16 Perpetua Roman at
SÜRYA

Printed and bound at
MicroPrints India, New Delhi

CONTENTS

In Memory

Bill Middleton and Monique Wittig

Acknowledgements

Several of these stories previously appeared in *The Georgia Review, The Pushcart Prize Anthology, Fence, The Barcelona Review, Press, Zyzzyva, Other Voices, The Missouri Review, Living in America, Hot Metal Bridge* and *The Alaska Quarterly Review.*

The Good Poet of Africa

A FRESH COAT OF WHITE PAINT FAILED TO OBSCURE THE OLD CRACKS on the office walls where the ambassador sat behind his desk in all his fleshy bulk, his rough, ungainly hands wiping the sweat from his face with whatever was closest: a corner of his jacket, the report on our prospects for the oil deal, the photograph of his only daughter. Behind him, the map of India nailed to the wall still owned to a vestigial East Pakistan, and next to this, portraits of Gandhi, Indira, Nehru and Rao hung like long-forgotten family members.

I yawned. He told me I was promoted, eating as he talked, that my transfer was imminent, laid a samosa back on his plate, and grimaced. The effort made his stomach pulse lightly up and down. I thought of him naked, riding his stick-like wife, eating all the while.

They were sending me to San Francisco, to the consulate there, though why, he didn't know, and saying that he laughed, a real crack-up of a laugh. Flecks of samosa shot across the desk, landing on reports and visa applications and even on the photograph of his wife. He recovered and wiped the photograph with a jacket sleeve. 'You have important friends,' he told me. 'Very high.' The fan ached above us, groaning from its constant, but useless, effort and a flutter of his fingers indicated the end of the meeting. He turned and picked up a stranger's passport and pressed it against his forehead, complaining that his constitution was unfit to handle many more years of this African climate.

That evening, in my room, with my shirt sticking hungrily to my back, I could think of no friends who might vaguely be considered high. My mind occupied itself with the memory of the ambassador's mass, the heat, and how, at this time of night, trucks passing in the street outside hummed with restless activity, as though the late hours had brought out in their engines a spirit of relentless and undirected motion.

A young Sikh greeted me in the terminal at SFO. Handsome, tall, with a clean, neat beard, bright eyes, a precisely arranged orange turban, he slapped me with comradely affection, a jolly, thick-fingered Punjabi slap. My new assistant, Bhagwant. Call him Baggie, he said, hauling two heavy suitcases, one in each hand. 'See. I'm really Baggie now.' The Consul was dying to meet me, he assured, but that would be later. He laughed, almost squealing, then abruptly stopped and apologized. It was an honour, he explained, to be asked to meet me at the airport. I concluded he must be an idiot and scrutinized the terminal, hoping someone else was hunting for me. But there was only Baggie who staggered beside me with an irrepressible grin and the gait of a drunk gibbon.

The next day, insisting I get to know the city, Baggie

pushed me onto a visitor's bus and left me stranded, crushed against the window by the elbows of a white-suited tourist. The man asked my name and I answered by silently raising the corner of my lip in a putative snarl. He turned quickly away.

This new home offered an unlikely intimacy. The irregular street plan, how hills first concealed a vista and then presented narrow, elongated views of streets and the bay beyond, the sense of motion and life, not undirected as it felt in Nairobi, but appearing purposeful—all contributed to a feeling that I could find a place here. When the bus arrived at the top of a hill, it afforded a view of the ocean. I realized I had not lived so close to a coastline since childhood. I twisted my neck as the bus turned a corner, attempting to catch one last glimpse of the blade edge of water.

Stepping off the bus, full of nostalgia for the ocean of my childhood, I confronted a wan noon heat and fell instantly against a young black woman who, had I not actually touched her, I would have said wasn't there. She held out a sheaf of purple flyers and, though it appeared she should be distributing them, simply stood there, consumed by the rising currents of hot exhaust from the bus. One hand was stretched forward in a gesture of apathy while her eyes remained sunk in boredom. I snatched a flyer and hurried on.

Come hear the Unities of East and West, the purple sheet announced, *of North and South. How we are all One World under the Benign Gaze of Atatatata.* The sheet listed a series of dates and times. I folded it into quarters and slipped it into my pocket. If she had said anything I would have discarded the paper immediately, but her silence and the sheet's curious message erased all thoughts of childhood and determined me to learn more about this Atatatata. All afternoon I remained under the spell of the studied apathy of her gaze.

The Consul was not as eager to see me as Baggie had earlier asserted, and several weeks passed before I received a summons. In the meantime I became increasingly accustomed to the spaciousness of my office and to the day's routine.

On one wall hung a portrait of Gandhi and on another, one of Singh. I was tempted to turn both around, but didn't, more out of torpor than fear of consequences. In the mornings, Baggie invariably asked what there was to do, though he almost certainly knew the answer far better than I. No doubt an inherent defect in his character kept him cowed. I despised him considerably more when he became personal, asking what I had done the previous evening.

My response was always curt, offered with a sneer, something like this: 'Why don't you make some tea, you know, real tea, chai, and cut your hair or something.' Nothing offended him, as if within him rested an indefatigable reservoir of simplicity and good nature, and it gave me rare pleasure to push up against the dams of that basin with what already felt like a hatred that grew out of some long ago and unresolved conflict.

My days filled themselves. The position was some species of cultural attaché, though no one confided my exact title, and I appeared charged with meeting any of the public who wanted to know more about India or Indian culture. A ludicrous post, as I knew little about India and cared less for it. Men and women of all ages were announced by Baggie and sat themselves down. Often I had no idea how to respond to their questions and so resorted to invention or vague generalizations. 'India is a large country and jam-packed with diversity!' The sort of thing people think they want to hear. One young woman dressed in red leather and expensive-looking torn jeans asked about the rave scene. I didn't know what a rave was and gave her a lengthy explanation of the many ascetics who dance in the streets, naked most of them, begging for a single bowl of rice. 'One day every year all India becomes like this. Everyone naked and dancing, begging for rice.' She looked excited when she walked out, and I pictured her stepping off the plane into a Delhi summer, her eyes intent on searching out a naked and frenzied India.

If they stayed long, especially women, I offered tea and sweets and tried to keep them talking while I sat there, imagining them in the nude, my pants inflating and collapsing with the slow passage of the day.

It was Baggie who drove me across the bridge one afternoon to help me buy a car. My choice was something large and flashy, an ancient DeSoto, with an engine which, when I turned the ignition, shook with a threatening and vibrant rattle. Baggie didn't understand my preference. There were many newer models, he said, much more reliable. 'You're not on an African salary anymore,' he declared in a tone that was curiously protective and, for the first time, my attitude toward him began to soften.

All warm feelings vanished when he suggested I join him

that night at his apartment. Every Thursday he hosted informal poetry readings. It was a group of his friends. They read old and new Urdu ghazals—always Urdu. Baggie claimed it was the real language of poetry.

I told him I hated poetry—worst was Urdu poetry. I had never seen him look so shocked.

That evening I found a note slipped under the windshield wiper of my new car. On it, Baggie had written his address and the dates and times of his salons. I laughed at his tenacity and felt oddly gratified at having an assistant like Baggie. That didn't stop me from crushing the paper into a ball and throwing it onto the floor of the passenger seat.

The night I visited the address listed on the purple flyer with its promise of benign divinity, a man answered the door, tall, muscular, and welcomed me with a handshake so hard I felt the sting in the bones of my palm for minutes after. His name was Dr Geronimo Boyce III. The tone of his voice was regular and precise and seemed, oddly, to originate not from his mouth but in the empty space between us, as if disembodied.

The young woman I'd met my first afternoon in San Francisco sat on a frayed couch, wearing bright yellow headphones, and chose not to acknowledge me when I walked in. Her expression seemed almost identical to that earlier glimpse I had caught.

On the walls, those not crowded with bookcases, hung African masks and artifacts. Similar ones overpopulated the tourist stalls in Nairobi. Here, the wooden faces stared down with menacing, uncertain expressions, incongruous within this studious and musty room.

'This is Aime Love.' Dr Boyce gestured vaguely in the direction of his daughter. When he spoke he did not look at me but rested his eyes on a spot in the air, as though addressing a fourth, spectral individual. 'Get it? Aime Love. Aime is Français for love, and with her last name being Love, she is really Double Love or Love Squared.' Double Love pulled the headphones from her ears and, in a voice long ago drained of all enthusiasm, asked her father to shut up.

'But, Love,' Dr Boyce offered, 'he doesn't know your special nature or how you came into this world filling it with joy.' Dr Boyce turned to me and I could see from his blank eyes that he believed every word he said. 'My friend, when Aime was born she was so full of the wonder and joy of life that we thought it a crime to call her anything else. Love wasn't enough to encompass her shining character, so we decided on Aime Love. Doesn't it suit her?' I nodded, unsure what else to do, and looked back at Double Love. Her eyes smouldered.

No one else arrived that evening, and throughout the night Dr Boyce walked continuously, making the precise figure of an eight around the two couches where Double Love and I sat facing one another. The old carpet revealed the frayed path of hundreds of such figure eights, perhaps thousands. His eyes unfailingly searched out that other, fourth person, only rarely coming to rest on me. Double Love had brought me a mug of coffee from the kitchen. She drank from one herself.

'I,' Dr Boyce announced, 'am the Seventh Avatar of Atatatata. Your people have avatars also, but they are false.

Atatatata has given them to you not to deceive you, but to prepare you for the knowledge of the real avatars, the Avatars of Atatatata.' Atatatata emerged from the love cauldron of Venus, Dr Boyce explained, where he had spent eternity balancing a rock on his nose and thimbles on his eyelash hairs. He came down to Africa where he consummated his marriage to the Earth with all types of animals, and from these different unions were produced different races—Neanderthals, Pygmies, Tibetans, Andorrans, the Welsh, Liberians, Sikhs. He droned on and soon my eyes fell back on Double Love, whose face had not moved and whose eyes registered an emotion lost between rage and lethargy.

The Seventh Avatar, without changing the rhythm of his speech, stepped into the kitchen to refill my cup. His voice continued, but the moment he was out of sight, Double Love started forward on her sofa. 'When he quits, don't leave. There's a side door. Follow the stairs up. My room is at the top.' She fell back instantly and soon her father returned carrying the coffee. Her expression remained unchanged, as if, during the moments the Seventh Avatar was out of the room, nothing had happened.

The attic ceiling of Double Love's room sloped at an acute angle. I ducked and stood stooped with Double Love's back to me, her face visible in the mirror of a low bureau where she sat examining herself. The room was scattered with clothes and tapes, and a single mattress rested on the floor. Minutes passed before she twisted around in her chair to acknowledge me after arriving at some moment of satisfaction with her own appearance. She swore at her father. 'How can you sit there? All those hours.' I was waiting to ask her the same question. 'Me?' she said and laughed. She shook her head. 'Me.'

In minutes, I was on top of her, and what surprised me was how stagnant and unresponsive her body remained. Her apparent hatred of her father had led me to believe the opposite would be true, but she was little more than a dead thing underneath me.

When it was over she found a cigarette and lit it and told me to put my pants on. 'You've got to leave,' she said, exhaling smoke into the tight, airless room, not bothering to offer me a drag. I descended the stairs without fuss and outside in the cold nighttime street I thought about her body and how she had lain there, motionless, on the threadbare carpet. I had done little more than mount her.

The following morning I shouted at Baggie. That thing on his head he called a turban was a disgrace, if he didn't know how to wrap one properly, what was he doing being a Sikh. He stared back at me, disturbed, so I told him to get out and not come back until he looked decent.

The early hours passed with the usual mixture of mild fantasies and, later, when Baggie returned with his turban straighter than a turban could possibly be, I found myself in a better mood. The Consul wanted to see me. 'He is eager,' Baggie said. Three weeks since my arrival and finally the Consul was displaying his eagerness. I laughed but Baggie didn't understand.

The Consul's office stood at the top of a wide flight of stairs, along a narrow corridor with doors on all sides and behind double wooden doors. This section of the consulate was alien territory as I'd kept my wandering circumscribed, having no desire to know more than I needed to fill my days. Noises emerged from behind the doors—pitched and delicate music, deep, exasperated groans, a fist striking wood, and even the sound of a chisel on stone. At the Consul's door, I could smell the pakoras, freshly made, that awaited me inside.

He was a thin man, unusual in the service, unheard of at his level. There was one unbreakable rule and he had broken it: the higher the diplomatic office achieved, the wider one grows, constantly ballooning and rising. He wore a plain Indian shirt, which only accented his boniness. The office was large but spare and, when he motioned for me to step forward and sit, he did so disinterestedly, not looking at me but beyond, down the hall and through the open door. Several miniatures in the old Mughal style hung on the walls, while in one corner a sitar took up residence.

'I trust you have settled in.' His voice was sharp and strong, not at all what I had expected from his appearance.

I nodded.

'Yes, yes, and you have been here . . .' His voice trailed off.

'Three weeks.'

'Yes, yes.' His eyes signalled the pakoras. I took one and dipped it into the chutney and ate it slowly. He didn't eat.

'How do you find it?' He twisted his head away from me and closed his eyes as though in contemplation of something distant and great.

'Find what?'

'The city, the job. All this.' He motioned with his hands to the room.

'The usual.'

There was silence for some seconds.

'You know I asked for you.'

'Asked for me?'

'Yes, yes. To come here from Africa. You are the poet, yes?'

'The what?'

'You are the poet. The good poet of Africa.'

I suppressed a laugh. Obviously someone had grossly misinformed him. I was not a poet. I never had been one. I hated poetry. He appeared disturbed but told me that clearly I was lying. 'You poets are recluses and no doubt don't like to be known, but this is going too far. Too far.'

An untidy stack of papers sat on his desk. He now picked several of these up and I saw that they were fax transmissions. 'These are yours, yes?'

The paper was thin and glossy and the writing, in Urdu, was poorly transmitted, some illegible. The office had received streams of such poems. Other embassies in the city also received them. All carried my name and all originated in Nairobi. I paged through them without interest. There was my name, scrawled in someone else's hand. All looked like dreary love poems, desire, loss, the usual sentimental ambit. I could care less.

'We got phone calls from all the consulates and embassies in the city asking who this phantom Indian poet was who lived in Nairobi.'

I dropped the pages onto the desk and shook my head. Someone was playing a trick, I said. The Consul was not convinced. Everyone here was an artist of one sort or another. The Consul himself, though not an artist, was a critic of the early Mughal style in painting. He waved his hand at the miniatures on the walls. 'Don't hide yourself. We know it was you. You must write more like this.' He pressed his finger down onto the stack of faxes. 'That is why I gave you an assistant. Think of those days in Nairobi as an apprenticeship. Now you at last have the ease to spread your wings. Your assistant can do your work, yes?'

I started to laugh. 'Is this why I was transferred?'

'Of course!'

I could think of nothing else to say. The whole situation was ridiculous. 'I'm not a poet,' I said finally, my voice flat.

'Do not lie to us.'

I stood and found that I was shaking. The tone of the Consul's insistence made me angry, and I clenched a fist as I walked out, saying only that I had an appointment.

The corridor met me with silence. Behind every door were hidden mouths no doubt sunk in scorn and laughter. Perhaps the joke had not originated in Nairobi but here. Perhaps someone here wanted to make a fool of me. I clattered noisily down the wooden stairs.

A teenager waited for me in my office. He was no more than sixteen, a high school student, and writing a paper on the history of languages for an honours history class. Could I tell him something of the Indian languages? I clapped my hands. Of course! For half an hour I fed him nonsense. All

Indian languages, I explained, were derived from Hebrew. 'That's where Hindi comes from. Notice how Hebrew and Hindi sound alike.' I was gratified to see him scribbling. Hebrew was a Dravidian language and therefore all Indian languages were also Dravidian. 'King David's original name,' I said, 'was Dravid. Thus, Dravidian.' All except Punjabi and Jain, which were invented by rajas for the sole use of eunuchs. 'All modern Punjabis and Jains are the descendants of eunuchs.' He wrote furiously.

With the so-called honours student gone, I exploded into spasms of laughter and Baggie popped his head around the door to ask what was so funny. I told him and he looked at me crossly, like an angry mother, and slammed the door on his way out. My thoughts returned to the current problem: who was it who might have worked alongside me in Nairobi, who might be here, scribbling those dreadful lines? I thought of those love poems sent across continents in seconds, the very handwriting of the writer, anonymous and electronic, a pulse on phone lines, a transmission from one satellite to another, drowning the sky—the whole spectrum of electromagnetic bands—in the hieroglyphs of miserable and repetitive passions.

The next morning found me having drunk a half bottle of bourbon, cotton-headed from a hangover, and curiously exhilarated on sighting Baggie with his downcast eyes. My assistant was still angry over the trick I played on the kid, and I told him I got drunk to celebrate, that's how good a joke it was. In the afternoon, Double Love was announced. 'A Miss Love,' Baggie's voice crackled over the intercom. Across her eyes I recognized that same torpid lustrelessness I had seen at her father's house. She wore a tight black skirt that stopped above her knees and a white tanktop and held a leather jacket slung over one shoulder. Before Baggie could close the door, she had thrown the jacket violently onto the desk and kicked off her shoes.

'It's so boring out there. He makes me stand there handing out that shit. God, I hate him.'

Her anger invigorated me and I was flattered she had come to see me. Our sex was hurried and anxious, performed standing up, her body pinned to the wall under the portrait of Singh. She was quick and unenthusiastic and, when she left, I noticed how her odour clung to me. I settled back into my chair behind the desk and replayed the feel of her body as it pressed against my skin and hands. When she had come, I was sure the hint of an expression had glimmered on her face. That memory stayed with me for days.

She returned the following week, and soon she was visiting every few days, sometimes three times a week. Always at the office, never where I lived, though I told her where that was. She preferred the cool afternoons, and we made love with increasing regularity. With each visit I detected a larger crack in the façade of her apathy. I wanted to break the mask completely. With her gone, I thought about her constantly. My body ached after the increasing violence of her movements and the diversions that normally propelled me through the days—my fantasies and tricks—lost their appeal.

I confessed this to her one afternoon. We were sitting together against the wall in the office, our bodies glistening from the sweat of our exertion, drinking tea Baggie had carried in on a tray. I no longer cared what he thought, yet I discovered there was something irreducible about Baggie's good nature. His anger never persisted long and soon he had grown used to Double Love's presence and prepared tea for her with extra sugar and not so much milk, the only way she said it did not totally disgust her.

I was in my underwear and she in a shirt whose flaps hardly covered the triangle of her crotch. Baggie now grinned on repeating his claim that I was corrupted within and without. Only rarely did his face cloud with worry on looking at me, but such times I ignored, and instead I experienced a growing fondness for Baggie and his ways. In a certain fashion he had become a regular aspect of my afternoons with Double Love.

I told Double Love I wanted her to come live with me. She immediately turned away and said it was impossible.

She hated her father and hated living there. Every moment was one of boredom and tedium. It was the straightforward solution, I argued. We would live together, in the same small room, and I would work and she would do exactly as she pleased, whenever she pleased. She shook her head and said she couldn't explain. I pressed her for a reason. I took her face in my hands and turned it toward me and demanded to know why. After a minute, she confessed that if she left her father, he would kill her. She was sure of it. He had done it before. He had killed her mother. When her mother tried to leave, he shot her. 'He made it into an accident. He spent a year inside for manslaughter. That's when he discovered who he was.' She laughed scornfully. 'The Seventh Avatar!'

Several days passed before I saw her again and I was given time to think over her confession and the Seventh Avatar's crime. After work one afternoon, I purchased a gun at an antique store south of the city, the kind I remembered from old westerns, with a silver barrel and a dark leather handle and a solid weight to it. Once home, the gun felt strangely light in my hand. When I bought it, I had no clear purpose, only guessing a gun might somehow help me free Double Love. Now I could protect her. That night I loaded the gun and slept easily with it close by on my bedside table.

I picked up a bottle of bourbon before work and opened it in the car. Baggie looked at me with concern when I walked in—he could smell the alcohol. By the early afternoon, when Baggie knocked to tell me I was wanted upstairs, I was drunk. The Consul again.

I allowed a half hour to pass before I stood and made my cautious way to the Consul's office. Along the corridor the same sounds echoed—faint strains of music, a chisel on stone, a man beating a desk. It occurred to me that I had seldom encountered my co-workers. The few I'd met appeared the dour and quiet fellows indigenous to diplomatic postings, except that here, the bustle of other consulates was absent, as was the morning rush when employees gathered to chat over tea.

The Consul offered me a jalebi but I refused. The bright orange sweet looked distasteful after the whisky. In the corner, instead of the sitar, stood a white marble statue of a hermaphrodite with a thick, erect penis and rounded breasts. The Consul's desk was free from the pile of papers that had littered it previously.

'So what of it?' he asked immediately.

'What?'

'How goes it? The work and all.'

'Very well. I saw five people yesterday and—'

'Yes, yes—that's not what I asked. The poetry. No one comes here to work. We do other things. The poetry. How does it go?' He violently thumped the desk with his index finger.

I looked at him with hatred. 'It doesn't,' I said as bluntly as I could. 'I am not a poet.'

He breathed in loudly through his nostrils and let his head fall back. He sat like this for some moments, examining the ceiling, eyes rolling from corner to corner as if seeking inspiration in such a truncated vision of heaven.

'Your ghazals are fine, modern ghazals. Some of the finest. When I read them I thought of Faiz.'

I responded derisively. 'Why did you bring me here?'

He looked back at me and for a moment appeared genuinely puzzled. 'To write, yes. Why else?'

I dropped my head into my hands. It felt pointless to protest further.

'I thought maybe seeing all your poems on my desk made you shy, so I have hidden them this time.' He pulled open a drawer and there appeared again the many faxes. He started to read. It was atrocious and I insisted that he stop.

'Why?'

His incomprehension touched me. His motive truly was an uncomplicated one. He had brought me here to write, like an ancient Khan who gathered around him the writers and artists of his time.

'I did not write those. I could not have. Didn't you get my file? I am a drunk. I am drunk. Now. I have the lowest rating in my office. Probably the lowest in the whole service. No one dared promote me.'

'Yes, yes. I know. But you poets are like that. We have a tabla player. One of the best here on the West Coast. He beats his wife and children and every now and then the police take him away for a few days. But he is a tabla player.'

I wanted to hit him now. He had begun to resemble the ambassador in Nairobi—if I poked hard enough I was sure he would burst. In a single gesture, I threw my arm across the desk and snatched the few poems he held in his hand; then standing, I tore them violently and scattered the fragments over the desk and floor. He rushed forward, surprised, and tried to stop me.

'There! That's the only poetry I'm capable of!'

Soon he was on his knees frantically gathering the pieces of paper. 'You don't understand!' he shouted. 'You can write here!' His pleas followed me out through the door.

In the corridor I heard steps hurrying toward me. It was Baggie, he was running and breathless.

'What is it?' I demanded.

'That boy's father is here.'

'Who?'

'That boy. Remember, the one you told all the tales to. The father is screaming downstairs. I couldn't keep him out of your office.'

'Come on,' I said. I walked quickly past Baggie and down along the corridor. His footsteps echoed mine and arriving at my office I didn't hesitate throwing the door open with a thrust of my hand and walking inside.

He was a tall man with short blond hair and I was struck by how much he resembled his son. They both displayed an arrogant air about their eyes, their noses sleek and elegant. His cheeks were red and I could see the simmering fury in his face.

'Was it you?' His voice was deeper than his son's, and it carried in it the familiar menace of weak but violent men. I knew immediately he was no match for me.

'Who told your son stories? Yes.' I walked across to my desk and casually picked up a file that lay among my papers and pretended to study it.

'Do you know what you did?'

'I can't imagine. Why don't you tell me?' I didn't look at the man.

'The teacher threw him out of the class. This was an honours class. He was going to go to Stanford. I went to Stanford.' He spoke with a metered determination at the end of which I knew waited a fist.

'The teacher told him if he couldn't take his papers seriously he obviously wasn't cut out for the honours program. They threw him out of all the honours classes. You ruined him.'

'Your son didn't deserve to be in that class. He should have checked out what I told him. That kid was stupider than he looked.'

Much to my joy, he raised a fist and prepared to strike. As he did so, the door burst open and Baggie charged in with two guards. The man stood motionless for a brief second and before the guards reached him, I had time to get a punch in. My fist landed square on his face and he fell back scrambling for balance and crying out in pain. The guards took hold of him and carried him out while he kicked and swore.

'I know your name,' he shouted from the doorway, trying to fight his way free. 'I'll be waiting for you.'

I could still feel his face on my fist. I'd been cheated from a real fight. I turned to Baggie. 'Who asked for your help?'

'That man is a maniac.'

For a moment I thought of striking Baggie, but turned away and told him to get out.

I took a drink of the bourbon and felt for the pistol in my briefcase. There it was and now was the time. Swinging the briefcase wildly, I walked out telling Baggie to cancel all appointments for the rest of the day. If Double Love came by, I told him to keep her occupied. 'Give her tea and read her ghazals.' His eyes telegraphed turmoil and confusion, but thankfully he said nothing, and I was able to escape without resorting to explanations.

The drive to Dr Boyce's house had me speeding through several stop signs. In the daylight, I saw how close the building stood to the ocean. The water stretched at the end of the road and a breeze swept along the street.

The pistol felt like a toy when I pulled it from my briefcase. It was hard to believe it could kill. I thrust it into my inside pocket where it pressed hard against my lung.

Dr Boyce smiled when he took my hand and said he was always glad to meet with a disciple of Atatatata. He looked smaller than I remembered and walked like an old man, and his joints appeared stiff from arthritis.

Nothing was changed from my previous visit, except for Double Love's absence, and I took a seat on the same sofa while the Divine Avatar prepared coffee in the kitchen. The air of mustiness mixed with the aroma of recently burned incense. A faint haze of smoke hung lazily in the room.

Soon the doctor was talking, as he had before, about the coming union of East and West, having shown no interest in why I'd come. In reality, he explained, there was no such thing as East or West. 'You stand in China and what is to the east? America. We are the Chinese east. And you stand on the coast here in California and it is Japan that is our west.' His voice sung crisply from the kitchen and, on returning with the coffee, he resumed his familiar peregrination around the room, forming the same, simple figure eight while his eyes searched the corners and the masks and the books for that other, spectral guest. The bright afternoon light revealed a heavy coating of dust burying all his possessions.

Taking a sip from the coffee, I placed the cup on the table and pulled the gun out from under my coat. It was best to end this quickly, in case anyone else should arrive, or I should lose my resolve. I didn't know what to expect when Dr Boyce saw the gun, but the last thing was that he would simply continue his figure eight, talking as if nothing had changed. Even the rhythm of his speech remained unaltered. 'There will come a time,' he said, 'when the West will have taken so much from the East and the East will have taken so much from the West that the one will become the other. East will be West but West will be East.' I raised the gun and pointed it at him, following him with the barrel. Still, he did nothing. His body passed so close that if I hadn't pulled the gun away his thigh would have struck it.

'That is when the Divine Atatatata will make his appearance.'

Then I understood: he was blind.

I waved the gun in the air as he passed by, making sure it crossed his field of vision. No reaction. There I sat, following him with the gun for several minutes, not knowing what to do.

Finally I asked what I had wanted to ask all along. Did he really kill his wife?

The question brought a pause from Dr Boyce and he turned toward my voice, not in the least surprised. 'Yes,' he said. 'It was because of me she died.'

I cocked the hammer of the pistol and prepared to squeeze the trigger.

'If I had not married her,' he continued. 'If I had not wanted a child.'

'What?' I said, holding the pressure firmly on the trigger.

'She died giving birth. Twenty years ago.'

Then, searching among the objects in that small room, I saw what I had not seen before. Not one photograph of Double Love showed her with her mother, though several showed Dr Boyce with his wife, a young couple starting out. Not proof, for sure, but right then that wasn't what I needed. I released the pressure on the trigger and dropped the gun into my lap. My body began to shake and I no longer knew what to do. What was it that I wanted? Dr Boyce continued his ramble around the room, unaware of what had just occurred.

Double Love was standing on the sidewalk, leaning against my car. She saw the gun in my hand and looked into my face. I don't know what she read there.

'Did you do it?' she said, as I ran down the steps toward her. She revealed little emotion, neither hope nor fear, but a generic lack of curiosity used when asking about the lives of distant, little known relations, and maybe a sense of trepidation.

'What?'

She pointed to the gun. 'I was hoping—' she said but broke off and turned away. 'I hear him calling,' she said, indifferently, showing no concern at discovering he was still alive. She frowned. 'I guess I've got to go.' She climbed the stairs but stopped before reaching the door.

'You can live here,' she called out from the top of the steps. 'Like me. Pretend this is home.'

Her voice was empty of animosity or affection, containing only the unpolished tone of that young woman whose name I had learned the first day I entered their house. What I had heard as trepidation moments before I now imagined as something else. She knew me better than I knew myself.

I pressed the gun into my pocket and, saying nothing, hurried down the street and toward the ocean, while behind me I sensed her eyes following me from the stoop with the same unvarying attention with which she might follow a plastic bag tossed violently in the air by the wind.

On the coast road, early rush-hour cars blasted their horns as I ran across the weather-beaten blacktop. The rays of sun sliced across at a sharp angle over the Pacific and my movements soon slowed as I progressed across the sand toward the water. Wading up to my waist, I remembered myself as a child doing exactly this. Crests foamed against my shirt and I experienced the fleeting excitement of a possible life, a different life, with Double Love and Dr Boyce, living right at the ocean's edge. Here I could run in the mornings and swim, and in the evenings sit with Double Love while we listened to her father's madness unfurl through the long and lonely nights.

When I pulled the gun from my pocket, the sun glinted off the silver barrel. I flung it as far as I could, watching it arc against the sky then become lost, almost instantly, in a rising white swell. It appeared again for a moment, a crisp, black shape amid the waves, and then was gone forever. When I turned to make my passage back toward the beach, I saw that a small crowd had gathered some distance along the edge and were staring at me with suspicion and fear. Someone would no doubt call the police and with that thought I felt myself jolted back into the world—the possible life vanished as quickly as I had conjured it.

I waded through the water and every step was a struggle. Only now did the cold hit me as I progressed back up the beach and toward the road. This time, I chose to wait for a break in the traffic. Double Love was gone from outside her house. I climbed into my car and dropped my head onto the steering wheel, exhausted and shivering.

The sun settled below the sharp horizon and I drove several miles south along the coastal highway. The skyline was red and the clouds were streaked across the western sky.

The night had settled in when I drove back into the city, and soon I found myself pulling up half a block from my apartment. A figure stood under the streetlamp near my building's door. I recognized the disgraced boy's father from the way he shifted his weight from one leg to another. All fight had fled me and I could not face the man. I doubted I would ever be able to face him again. I started the engine and the car jerked to an anxious, uncertain life and I drove away.

At a stop sign, I reached across to the passenger seat and searched the floor until I found the scrap of paper I was looking for. It was Baggie's address, and with it the dates and times for his evening salons.

Before I had a chance to ring the bell, I heard Baggie's voice emerging from an open window. I waited and listened as he recited one poem after another. Something horrid in Urdu, but instead of laughing I was filled with a pathetic gratitude. I wasn't home, I never would be, but for a moment, I was sure, Baggie would help me pretend. I felt a surge of relief at the prospect of sitting with him, listening to his poetry and imagining myself as another man in another age, the good poet of Africa the Consul once believed I was. Wet and shivering, I pulled my jacket tight around me and climbed the final steps to his door. Right then I recognized a line Baggie spoke and froze. Soon there was another and after that another, and I knew where I had seen those lines before. The world was funnier than I thought, and a host of new questions pestered me as I reached forward and pressed the bell.

The Discovery

THE WOMAN'S MOUTH WAS ROUND AND SOFT, A GLAZED DOUGHNUT of a mouth smeared in scarlet frosting. I dreamed of her lips clamped to my chest—they were a suction cup, leaving only a ring of red and a vacuum to separate us. I drifted happily on the fantasy until she said something that should have disturbed me. I was only half-listening, and the jolt faded as quickly as it arrived. I never watched the tail-end news. The sportscast was over and all that was left were the human interest stories. The woman's lips were stuck to my chest, her saliva dripped through the TV screen and found a natural home in the jungle of my nipple hairs. I only heard the words *breaking news* as an aside to her teeth biting my nipple, only caught the splintered bodies falling from the plane in the reflection on an imagined ruby blood bead as her teeth pierced my skin. *Sikh terrorists,* she said. My hand found my crotch, and slowly, I unzipped my pants.

The next morning, the newspaper lying motionless and folded on the kitchen table, a bland, emasculated exclamation point, the unease of the night before returned. There was something in the news I suspected I didn't want to read about, and, unaccountably, my hands were shaking when I unfolded the paper.

Instead of looking at the headline, I took the first short sip of coffee. Hot, almost scalding. My tongue retreated. But I had to laugh at the headline when I saw it. 213 DIE IN AIR INDIA CRASH. What an amazing mistake, a fabulous error. We had made up that name as kids. My sister and I playing in the backyard creating countries out of molehills. She had Czechoslovakia, a real country. And I made up India. Dreambirth country whose dry, California dirt borders were no more certain than a cowpat, for this was a yellow-grass-surrounded-India.

I scanned quickly through the story, hoping that perhaps there was only the single typo, the sole error. But the word repeated itself, again and again—Air *India*, *India*, *Indians*. With each repetition the newscaster's voice from the night before found an ugly path into my brain—*Sikh terrorists from the North Indian state of Punjab have claimed* . . . The word almost gave itself meaning, as though seeing it printed and repeated, the mirror image of a lie flashing endlessly, gave it a core of truth. But what responsibility could these terrorists have claimed? Killing not-Indians from not-India on an Air not-India. This must be a joke, some tremendous and ridiculous trick.

I walked into the other room, forgetting my coffee, and picked up the heavy tan phone from off the telephone book, and soon found the newspaper's number.

The assistant editor's voice was frantic, on edge about

something. I tried explaining my problem, in fact, my basic sense of confusion, in a slow, controlled tone so as not to disturb him further. It was no doubt a clerical error, a simple typo, a computer glitch. However, when I was about to say the word, or more correctly, the non-word, I found I couldn't get it out of my mouth. My lips were paralyzed, became rock and formed a high dam against the not-word.

'You say in your paper,' I said, 'that terrorists from . . .' I started again. 'A plane from . . .' The river of my speech was blocked mid-sentence.

'Are you talking about the Air India explosion, sir?'

'Yes . . . I mean, no.' I couldn't easily explain my dilemma. 'There was no explosion, there couldn't have been. There was no plane. There is no country. There are no people. No word.' Without saying a word, the assistant editor hung up on me.

I walked back into the kitchen and picked up the newspaper again. From the short drawer to the right of the stove I pulled out a pair of orange handled scissors. I clipped the non-word out of the headline, and out of every occurrence in the story and in the paper. As I searched through the pages, the word multiplied, it fractured and splintered, spreading like a fungus across almost every page. My hand was tired when I finished. On the table the shallow breast of clippings lay awkwardly, as though demanding something from me. I had nothing to give it. Only its negation.

The next day was Monday, and in the morning I telephoned the gas station I worked at. Without even a word of greeting, Sandeep, the manager, asked angrily where I was. Words vanished momentarily from my mouth.

'Is it that late?' I asked finally.

'You should be here an hour ago,' and then he swore at me in Gujarati. Speaking only Hindi and English, I didn't know what he said.

'Talk in English,' and I swore in Hindi.

'Don't you . . .'

I cut him off. 'Let me tell you. My aunt, she was in that plane yesterday. She died in that plane.' I lied.

Only the phone line hummed, vibrating in the expanding maw of space between us. I explained I would be out of town for the funeral, and added, 'I'll be in Delhi, in *India*.' I emphasized *notIndia*.

There was a sound like a vacuum filling with gas. Sandeep's breath yearned after that notword notIndia, as though it were real. I could hear his Adam's Apple gulping for a taste of that notcountry, shucking back and forth. He wanted it bad. Was I the only one who saw, who could hear, even over an old phone, this desire for an imaginary country, this hard-on for the unreal centrefold of notIndia? I slammed the phone down. No use.

My hands were shaking as I pocketed the orange handled scissors and left for the library. When I had created the notcountry, my sister had laughed and immediately took out a piece of paper. With a thick brown marker she wrote the notcountry in bold, shaky letters. We pinned the paper with a knitting needle to the spot where notIndia lay in our garden. It was a small, irregular molehill, surrounded by patches of crisp, yellow grass. It stood in one corner of the backyard, in a spot where the sprinkler never quite reached.

My sister and I threw stones as atom bombs at each other's countries, but each morning the countries were revived, had grown back from the ashes of their nuclear annihilation. No nuclear winter cast its long shadow over their phoenix-land plains. Until one night I crept out with a thick, palm-filling flashlight and kicked my sister's country down to the level of soil over an old grave. There was only India left. NotIndia, I mean.

The librarian's blonde hair fell in a sharp braid down the back of her neck. Her green pullover outlined her breasts as full-bodied molehills, and her smile showed a dull row of almost regular teeth.

'What do you mean?' she questioned, her smile fading, nuclear clouding over. I felt a chill of fear immobilize my mouth into wordless anxiety. 'The not country, India?' Her voice was direct and honest, a little loud for a library. Her questioning look gave me a moment's hope. Perhaps she didn't know the word. Perhaps she wasn't in on this massive hoax, this trick or joke or disease.

Then she said, 'We have some books on India. The country India. If that's what you mean?' I nodded and followed her silently across the floor. When she stood she was much taller than I'd expected, and her legs made long, arcing strides as she walked into the stacks. Behind her I felt small and worried. Distrust and not a little anger was growing in me. How could she know? How dare she know about my notword, my notcountry, my notIndia?

The stack on world history stood at the far back wall and the fluorescent tube overhead was out. The only illumination was the diffuse finger of light which came through a thin rectangular window set high in the adjacent wall. She pointed out the shelves on Asian history and politics.

'Here,' she said, 'this shelf is mostly India.' I saw the series of familiar names. Nehru, Gandhi, Lajpat Rai.

'My aunt, you know, is married to an Indian man,' she confided. Why I'm not sure. What did I care about her aunt's marrying a figment of my imagination. 'Perhaps you know him. Vishnu Patel.'

'No,' I said tersely, 'I don't know any Indians.'

When her long braid disappeared around the corner of the far stack, I knelt down and began inspecting more closely the shelf of books she had pointed out. *The Glory That Was India. India's Century. A Short History of India. Communism in India*. I could hardly believe it. Many of these books were old, decades old. Could this deception be so grand, so all encompassing? I paged through one book quickly, seeing the notword repeated over and over, almost at random, an electron-name whose position I couldn't predict—I could only know its orbit.

Carefully, making sure no one could see, I squatted down on the floor and took out the scissors hidden in my pocket. With a surgeon's precision I began cutting out each entry from the book, each time the notcountry, the notnationality, the notword appeared I made sure it found its way into my pocket. By the time the morning was over, I had four bulging pockets, and had gone through most of the books on the shelf. I couldn't touch the spines or covers unfortunately. I had to make sure it would be some time before my healing of these history books was discovered. I was still under the impression then that this was some passing madness, a flu on the political geography of the planet. That within a week it would pass, be spent, and that no one would ever mention the notcountry again. NotIndia would revert, as it had always been, to just a scrap of paper pinned to a Punjabi family's molehill in Fresno, California. Blowing in the hot, late summer wind.

At home, I spread the cuttings out across the small kitchen table. There were so many that I had to put some on the sparse counter space by the stove, next to my jar of masala and box of Stovetop Stuffing. I even laid some on the floor. Many had been crumpled in my pocket, and I spent a good hour trying to straighten or flatten some of the most damaged. This further complicated the kitchen, as between the neat, flat lying cuttings were groups weighted down and hidden beneath books, or flattened with plates or salt shakers at either end to keep them straight.

Soon after, I stopped watching TV or reading the newspaper. There were other notcountries. Even the newspapers acknowledged them. Creating them in one sentence and destroying them in the next. I learned that the notcountry notNorth Yemen was no more. That the notSoviet Union had fractured and splintered back into what it was. That notYugoslavia was, in fact, not. As was notEthiopia. Even my favourite newscaster, the woman whose lips I often imagined caressing my body or licking with soft, fish-like lips the tip of my penis, began sprinkling her speech with more and more notcountries and notwords.

My friends decided I was joking. 'Not India,' they'd laugh. 'Very good, Ranjit. It's the only way to get away from that bloody country, eh, just disappear it, make it dissolve. Very good.' They didn't believe me. Many talked about it as though it were real, as though under its umbrella it somehow sheltered all those places we had come from. NotIndia, I learned, was home to Punjab and Gujarat, Patiala and Delhi. Bombay was in notIndia, as was Bengal, and the Sutlej flowed into the Indus within the boundaries of an ancient notIndia. Some even spoke of visiting the notcountry, of returning permanently. I was horrified. 'Next year,' said Sunil, 'I'm going back for good. I'm leaving these damn goras to their own damn country. There's nothing here for us. Our home is India.' What could I do but bring him to my apartment. I had to show him.

'What is all this?' asked Sunil, his jaw dropping in what I thought at first was proper respect for the scale of the problem, of the spreading disease. 'Why all these words, all these cutouts?'

Everywhere, in my whole apartment, on tabletops and countertops, over every inch of floor and wall and ceiling. Words. Notwords, I mean. Even covering the slits of the toaster there was *Czechoslovakia* and *industrial*. I ate among the notwords, the notcountries and notverbs, notpeople. I drank my morning coffee staring at their nonexistence, drinking it in with every sip. When I sat on the sofa, I had to clear a space for myself, pushing the nots aside. Sunil didn't stay long enough for me to clear a space on the sofa for him. I wanted to say to him, not everything is covered. Not the sink, or the bathtub or the nottoilet.

He was gone before I could tell him, and I was left alone.

I have since stopped leaving the apartment. Sunil continues to visit and brings with him food. So much of it I can't eat, it isn't food. I don't know why he brings notfood. When I asked him not to, he shook his head. 'You must eat it,' he demanded with a madman's self-confidence in his own delusion. I knew he was sick and I questioned if I wanted to allow him entry anymore. Perhaps he would infect me. Perhaps the notwords would become words again. The thought terrified me. Notindia would become India, the notSovietUnion would reform.

There is little room left for food anyway, even notfood. There are more notwords than words in the world, and each day I find others. I am reduced to reading only the junkmail, and what Sunil sometimes leaves, a magazine or a newspaper, but it breaks my heart to open them. It's spreading, and there's nothing I can do about it. Soon there will be no room left, soon they will overflow, escape again, back, back . . . Where can I possibly put them all? My apartment is almost full. The bathtub is crowded, as is the nottoilet, and all the closets and all the sinks, and all my notplates and floors. Even under the bed, and all my jacket and trouser pockets. The house is swimming in them. On the rare occasions when I open the door, I shore up the clippings by forming a short storm wall in the hallway. It's the only way to stop them from spilling out onto the landing and escaping back into the world.

Recently I found a letter from my sister. I have no idea how long it sat among the clippings by the door. The postmark was from two months ago, and I don't know how it came here. It was clearly from my sister. Her name was in the top left corner, but even now I'm afraid to touch it. It's addressed to a notperson. I carefully cut the name out and pasted it to my front door. Through the small hole in the envelope I saw the green of dollar bills. I was sure I'd seen the notname other places. On a driver's licence I found in the kitchen drawer, and on a chequebook. Maybe he once lived here.

Good Indian Girls

On Tuesday night, Lovedeep returned for a second evening to the de-cluttering class she had, two weeks previous, persuaded herself would bring order to her life and aid in accomplishing a list of modest goals. Gain self-confidence. Find a better job. Fall in love.

'De-cluttering,' the flyer promised, 'empties more than the closet and the desk. It starts you on a road to shedding years of negative habits and self-sabotaging behaviour.'

The class was led by a rake-thin woman with close-cropped, blonde hair who sat Indian-style on a metal desk. The room was usually reserved for karate classes. Glossy posters lined the walls, outlining positions and moves. The early arrivals helped the instructor unfold stacked chairs and carry the heavy metal desk from the utility closet so as not to scuff the floors. Lovedeep was an early arrival, and before the first meeting, as she unfolded one chair after another and set it softly on the wooden boards, the instructor smiled privately at her. When she walked to the front to formally sign in, the instructor leaned in close and whispered, 'My heart is Indian.'

She had always wanted to go there, but never had. Except in past lives, of course.

'I've lived there before. I feel it in my blood.'

The confidence angered Lovedeep. She turned and walked hurriedly to a seat and looked out with studied indifference through the window. Beyond the rows of parked cars and the uniform line of trees shielding the highway, a deep blood red soaked the sky.

That night she dreamed of a naked old man in a cowboy hat hopping cross-legged from one feathery cloud to another while his knees streamed blood and his limp penis flopped menacingly between his hairy thighs. The dream must mean something and she told herself to write it down and think on it, though she never did, and a week later, trying to recall it, all she could remember was a floating cowboy hat taunting her from the heavens. The memory held an erotic charge, though why, Lovedeep could not say.

The first week's class had ended with a group meditation. Only by emptying the mind, the instructor said, could you successfully empty the closet.

Saying that, she began chanting. It was some sort of Indian-sounding nonsense. Lovedeep kept her eyes wide open the whole time out of a rising fury. When it was over, she told herself she would not return for the second week and instead would write a fierce letter of complaint to the school. In any event, she no longer required a second week. The most important of her goals was now considerably closer to being achieved.

She was on the road to falling in love.

He sat two rows in front during that first week, tossing his head absently from side to side, scratching his neck, and leaning back to yawn. Standing and turning to exit when the instructor announced the break, their eyes met and he grimaced at her. The grimace telegraphed both boredom and complicity. Lovedeep assumed he was equally irritated by the instructor's new age quackery.

Outside, in the parking lot of the strip mall, he told her his name. It was Ian. Amid high fluorescents shimmering against polished car bodies, the name sounded irresistibly exotic.

'Do you like it?' he said, nodding his head to indicate the class.

'The instructor's an idiot,' Lovedeep said. 'It's a waste of money. I don't know why I came.'

He nodded, saying nothing. He had driven from over fifty miles away, just for this class. He liked to get out of his own town, away from people who might know him.

'The highways are empty this time of night,' he said. It was as if he was revealing one of the secret laws of the universe.

Before the break was over, she had written her number on a torn corner of scratch paper and offered it to him. He stared at it, 'Lovedeep?' and thrust it into his trouser pocket. 'What kind of name is that?'

'Indian,' she said defensively.

'Oh.'

'Have you been there?'

'I've never thought about the place.' He spoke dully, with a lack of excitement, as if signalling he wasn't one of those guys hunting after the latest fad ethnicity to date and notch onto his belt of conquests.

After she handed him the phone number, his right hand began to shake visibly. 'Are you alright?' she asked.

He didn't know what she was talking about, and she told him that his hand was shaking.

'There's nothing wrong with me,' he said. 'It's not shaking, it's perfectly still.'

It began to shake more violently after he said that. His whole arm seemed to be undergoing a series of uncontrollable spasms.

'See,' he said.

He must be shy of his disability, she thought, and decided not to question him further.

'Oh, yes,' Lovedeep said. 'I can see it now. It's not moving. It must be the light.'

'There's a lot of people in India,' he said.

'There is.'

'A lot of people must die? People must die and no one cares?'

She had never thought about such an India before, an India of countless thousands dying every day. It conjured an image of bodies stacked on bodies, like the movies the first horrified GIs took of the concentration camps in Germany after liberation. In her mind, the stack of bodies grew ever higher, until the ground itself could no longer support the weight, and the continent sank into the warm southern waters under the pressure of so much dead flesh.

'It's a cruel place,' she said finally.

She followed him back into the class. All the while, his arm shook violently.

Lovedeep worked at a medical billing clearing house, passing bills from one vendor to another, double-checking for errors, cross-billing or overpayment, recommending recalcitrant accounts for collections action. The adjoining cubicle was occupied by Marjorie, whose job was similar, and though Lovedeep had been here for only two years, Marjorie had worked at the firm for eight. Why she had never applied for promotion, Lovedeep never asked and Marjorie never ventured. They worked at the end of a pointless L-shaped room, where the architect, perhaps having drawn himself into a corner, had left a sort of void. Few people ever had any reason to turn the corner where their desks sat together and say hello. Was this why they had become friends? Because fate had swept them both into this unpeopled hinterland?

Marjorie's desk was littered with bric-a-brac, photos, toys, the remnants of countless lunches swallowed while surfing the internet. New trash appeared daily, invisibly, as if Marjorie herself took no part in the accumulation, but that, having been washed down river, it reached her cubicle and found it could travel no farther. It stopped, having struck a dam. This thought disturbed Lovedeep. She feared she too would be consumed eventually, that the trash burying Marjorie's desk would overflow and fill hers, that together they would be drowned. It was because of this fear that she'd taken it upon herself to draw Marjorie out and become her friend, believing Marjorie's particular stagnation could be alleviated by companionship.

The day after the first evening of the de-cluttering class,

Lovedeep told Marjorie about Ian. Marjorie said she hoped he would call, and she wanted to hear all about it, but that Lovedeep should not get her hopes up. More damage had been done in the world by false hopes than by anything else, she said, though she did not elaborate on this statement with specific evidence. Lovedeep, despite noticing this lack, said nothing.

The class was held on Tuesday night, and therefore Lovedeep expected Ian to call on Thursday afternoon. She'd given him her landline number, not her cell, which she kept at the office. He would leave a message and she would call him back on Thursday evening, after she'd had a drink with Marjorie, and they would make plans for either Friday or Saturday night.

On Thursday afternoon, using her cell phone, Lovedeep dialled her home phone every quarter hour, expecting to find a message from Ian. Her spirits rose when she called for the seventh time and found the line engaged. Someone else was calling. Previously, the few times she'd found her phone engaged, she'd become afraid a burglar was at that moment sitting on her bed and making calls to his many overseas lovers and inviting all the other local felons over to ransack the apartment. Of course, it was always only her mother, asking if she was coming to visit that weekend or complaining about her father.

Still holding the phone to her ear while the busy signal beeped, she tapped the wall of her cubicle and Marjorie's head appeared. 'It's him,' Lovedeep said. 'He's leaving a message.' Marjorie nodded and made a motion to smoke a phantom cigarette and threw five fingers into the air. 'Right,' Lovedeep nodded, 'see you out there.'

A minute later, Lovedeep called home again. The message was from her mother.

She stood outside next to the sign reading SMOKING AREA and told Marjorie her father's knees were hurting again. 'Bad, is it?' Marjorie said and blew smoke into the air. 'Not very,' Lovedeep said. 'Mom worries.' Marjorie told a dirty joke about a priest with a bum knee, a young boy and a tuba player. Lovedeep never understood Marjorie's jokes but she always laughed as if she did. This time was no different.

Neither spoke about Ian's non-existent message.

Lovedeep decided this was done out of tact on Marjorie's part, but worried later if Marjorie simply didn't care. Because Lovedeep had spent so much time cultivating Marjorie's friendship, Marjorie was her only friend at work, but she remained troubled over whether Marjorie felt the same toward her as she did toward Marjorie. It was Lovedeep who telephoned Marjorie when the two were not at work, and it was Lovedeep who invited Marjorie to go out for happy hour on Thursday nights. The Thursday night happy hour included half-priced margaritas and complimentary personal pizzas and bread sticks. On Friday night, by comparison, only peanuts were on offer and the drinks were merely a dollar off.

Several weeks earlier, she had asked Marjorie why she never invited her to happy hour, and Marjorie said plainly, 'You say it first,' which was true. The following Thursday, Lovedeep decided to wait for Marjorie to say it first.

Her routine was to wait until after lunch, and on the Thursday of the experiment, Lovedeep was able to wait an additional twenty-seven minutes before she broke down and invited her friend to happy hour. But Marjorie had other plans that night, she had a date. 'When were you going to tell me?' Lovedeep said, barely able to conceal her hurt. 'I didn't know it mattered,' Marjorie said. 'I promise to tell you about it tomorrow.'

Tomorrow arrived and Marjorie said nothing.

This silence was the cause of no small resentment on Lovedeep's part, but she felt she could not quiz her friend, for Marjorie had promised, and asking would only raise the spectre of the broken promise between them. On the following Thursday, when it came time to ask Marjorie to happy hour that night, Lovedeep was unable to articulate the request. Her mouth froze and she stood before Marjorie's cubicle as if before a judge's chair, paralyzed, finding it suddenly difficult to breathe. A half hour later, the two women stood leaning against the stucco exterior of the building, smoking Virginia Slims, and Lovedeep listened as Marjorie spoke for ten uninterrupted minutes about a neighbour's dog that had barked all night long. It wasn't Marjorie's neighbour, it was a friend's neighbour's dog, and Marjorie's indignation was on her friend's account, not her own. Walking back inside, Lovedeep wondered, if a dog had kept her awake all night, would Marjorie's indignation have been equally forceful. It was not a question she wanted to find an answer to, and sitting back down, a weight descended on her. It was a feeling of dull nausea. Two photographs were pinned to the familiar faded pink fabric covering of her cubicle wall. In one, her mother stood in front of a life-size plaster statue of a giraffe with the paint peeling. In the other, her father supported a slice of cake and stared with sour embarrassment at the camera. Neither of her parents could remember where or when each was taken, and this small mystery had always excited Lovedeep. Not everything was known, things remained to be discovered, the universe still guarded secrets. Indeed, there were times she looked down at the piles of papers scattered across her desk: receipts, invoices, queries, letters, memos, printed out emails, threats for legal action, etc., and could not comprehend what they were. Even paper lost the quality of its paperness. At such moments, the world glowed with a tangible strangeness and danger. Anything might happen. She might fall madly in love. She might be brutally murdered. Both prospects thrilled her equally.

Marjorie tapped the divider and a moment later, her head appeared. 'Well?'

Lovedeep, her face upturned, stared wide-eyed. Since returning from the smoking break, the universe had lost its edge of unknowing. The photographs were mysteries only because her parents lacked the interest to trace the memories. The papers spread out in piles impinging on her keyboard were dull and self-explanatory. The colour of the fabric of her cubicle walls represented nothing more than a measurable wavelength of light. The world was what it was and nothing more and would forever remain exactly this.

Marjorie wanted to know if Lovedeep was going to ask her

to happy hour that night, because if Lovedeep wasn't, she'd have to come up with another plan, and quickly, as it was already late in the afternoon. Yes, Lovedeep had wanted to ask earlier, something had stopped her talking. Didn't Marjorie notice her friend standing there, nearly choking, trying to get the words out?

Marjorie winced. Was that what that was?

The flat screen television behind the bar was tuned to a news channel and on her third margarita, Lovedeep looked up to be confronted by a video close-up of a dead woman's face. The woman had been strangled.

'Another one?' Marjorie said.

'Is that number two or three?'

'Number three.'

The killer was known as the Internet Strangler because after each murder he released a video-nasty onto the internet of the dead woman's face. Nothing else, just a close-up running for as long as five minutes. The report excerpted a few seconds from the whole video and the stricken face of the newscaster returned. The music was loud in the bar and the television sound was switched off. The running subtitles for the deaf were largely incomprehensible due to the high number of spelling errors and typos. A composite sketch appeared, showing a round, balding head and a man with sleepy, humourless eyes.

Lovedeep decided he looked cute.

On her fourth drink and third free personal pizza, Marjorie confessed that last week she had lied when she said she had a date. She had wanted to do something different, by herself, maybe go to a different bar, maybe get picked up by a stranger, get fucked in the bathroom, that kind of thing. She didn't. She went home and watched television and, in the middle of the night, woke up in a fright, walked into the living room naked, switched on all the lights and opened the curtains, and took hold of her one potted plant and threw it out the window. It landed and shattered on a car's hood with a thundering crash. In seconds, an alarm started blasting.

'What happened?' Lovedeep was mesmerized.

Nothing happened, Marjorie said. After five minutes, the alarm went silent and in the morning, she woke, naked and sprawled in the living room as if the victim of a rape. She passed the car as she left for work. The remnants of the potted plant were still there and a dent bruised the hood. On her return in the evening, the car had vanished, and so had any sign of the plant.

Marjorie lit a cigarette and blew smoke into Lovedeep's face. Then she pulled back and grinned, and said, 'I'm sorry, I'm so sorry,' though it was unclear exactly what Marjorie was apologizing for. A lingering sense of discomfort followed Lovedeep to the women's room. It was here she first spotted the flyer taped to the wall, next to the mirror. 'CLOSET FULL? LIFE EMPTY?' the bold letters stated. 'Change your life. Throw out the old you. Start from scratch. Get moving today on the path to a clutter-free future.' She tore off one of the tabs with the phone number for information; then suddenly, as if possessed, ripped the flyer from the tiles and walked out. She slapped it onto the counter in front of Marjorie. 'I'm going to this next week,' she said. 'Do you want to come?' Marjorie's head was down, her fingers curled around the stem of a margarita glass. A minute passed before Lovedeep realized her friend was asleep.

The only reason Lovedeep returned for the second week of the de-cluttering class was in the hope of seeing Ian again. The same short-haired instructor sat cross-legged on the metal desk at the front of the room and started proceedings with a breathing and affirmation exercise. 'Imagine you are sitting in a garden surrounded by empty shelves,' she said softly. 'You hear a waterfall and see a closet with absolutely nothing in it. You are the closet. Say it to yourself, with each inward breath. Say, I am the empty closet waiting for life to fill me up.' Lovedeep kept her eyes wide open and remained furious while around her women mostly expanded their chests and breathed out noisily through their mouths.

Ian was nowhere, and she felt humiliated and cheated.

During the break, she confronted the instructor. Did she remember the man with the round head from last week, so tall, a little pudgy, with sleepy eyes? Yes, the instructor said, he was a weird one. She was glad he didn't come back. 'Bad vibes. Ugly, even. I'd stay clear if I was you.' Lovedeep decided the instructor was jealous. She plucked up her courage. 'Do you have his number?' she asked. The instructor took a moment to consider her response, took hold of Lovedeep's wrist and brought her mouth close to Lovedeep's ear.

'We're after bigger things, aren't we, you and I,' she whispered. Lovedeep didn't know what she was talking about. The instructor continued, 'We want to overturn our lives. Start from scratch, tear open our bodies.' The instructor's breath beat warmly against Lovedeep's ear. 'Listen to me, I know what you need. Come with me to India. Take me there. Please.'

The instructor's nails pressed into the flesh of Lovedeep's wrist. 'We can do it together, we can walk from the bottom of India all the way to the top.'

Saying that, her nails pressed so hard that Lovedeep let out a cry and wildly yanked her arm free. She turned furiously and started racing past the stunned eyes of her fellow students.

Behind her, the instructor called out her name.

Lovedeep slammed open the door and threw herself into the crowd of milling smokers and out into the parking lot with its warm air smelling of car exhaust. Once inside her own car, she burst into tears. The instructor was right. She wanted more than anything to overturn her life, to start anew, to become someone else entirely. She turned on the engine and drove away, thinking that she was nothing more than a coward.

A message was waiting on the answering machine. It was from Ian. On hearing it, all the agitation of the evening disappeared instantly.

He was sorry for not calling earlier. He'd planned to see her again at class tonight, but got delayed. Traffic. He was in the area. If she was up, could he come over? He wanted so much to see her. There was something he wanted to tell her, and he could only say it to her face.

The first thing he did on entering was to walk into her bedroom and open the closet doors. He was carrying a backpack and a small, black leather case that looked like a camera bag.

'It's not so bad,' he said, indicating the closet. 'You don't need that class.' He held up a wide leather belt and admired it. 'I like this. You should wear it.' He handed it to Lovedeep.

She had watched him walk from the door, across the living room and into her bedroom, with disbelief and a rising sense of admiration. She liked how he moved, he was familiar, it was as if he lived here already. Everything that had happened to her that day, these last few weeks, maybe even everything that had ever happened to her, had been erased when she heard his message. She was a different person already. Tomorrow, she would tell Marjorie this. 'I'm not your friend anymore,' she would say, 'I don't know why I ever was. Go find someone else.'

'The woman at the class told me you give off bad vibes,' she said to Ian. 'She said you're ugly. In spirit or something, I don't know.' She slipped the belt around her waist and pulled it tight.

'Tighter.' He pulled it tight for her. 'Like that.'

With the belt so tight, Lovedeep had trouble breathing.

'You're going fast,' she said. 'Let's have a beer. You did bring some.'

He pulled a six-pack out of the backpack. Coors. She hated Coors.

'My favourite,' she said, opening a can and following him back into the living room. A heavy glass ashtray sat on the coffee table, overflowing with butts. She lit a cigarette and offered it to him. He took it wordlessly.

The apartment was sparsely furnished. A sofa, loveseat, glass-topped coffee table, television. When a friend came over, they sat together, smoking, discussing what to order for takeout or watch on cable. Despite the lack of furniture, her experience of the room was of being suffocated. She could not walk, she told herself, without tripping over all her crap. Was this why she'd jumped at the opportunity when she saw the de-cluttering flyer in the women's room that night?

'How long have you lived here?' he said.

They were sitting together on the sofa. His hand was shaking again.

It took her a moment to remember. 'Two years.'

The room looked shockingly different with Ian in it. Gone was the clutter, the sense of suffocation. How little she really owned! How much space was there! The walls were bare, the shelves empty, yet for two years she had thought it crowded, almost uninhabitable. She owed him a debt for opening her eyes.

'People know you?' he asked.

'Not really.'

'It's good to be anonymous. Come and go as you want, no one poking their nose in.'

'What's in the camera bag?'

'A camera.' He laughed.

She finished the beer and opened a second. 'There's that guy going around killing girls and filming it,' she said.

'I know.'

'Have you seen the videos? They show bits on TV. Weird. Just the face.'

He placed a hand on Lovedeep's wrist and gripped it tightly. It was the same wrist the instructor had dug her nails into, but instead of the need she had felt in the instructor's touch, all she felt now was relief. He had shown her, just by walking into her apartment, how much space she really lived in.

'I like you,' she said.

He tipped his head back and closed his eyes and talked softly to the ceiling.

'It's beautiful,' he said.

'What is?'

'The face after death,' he said.

He spoke as if in a dream, and she wondered if the dream she'd had the night she met him was somehow connected to this moment, that perhaps he was the essence of that very dream made solid.

'Just lying there,' he continued, 'thinking nothing at all. You can think a lot of odd things staring at a dead girl's face. It makes the mind wander, clears the head of all that other bullshit, makes a man capable of seeing for miles ahead. A man could see straight to Arizona from here. You'd think it'd be nasty, but no. They're relaxed, they know the answers now, they've gone across, they've faced the last battle, and they've taken a little bit of you with them. That takes courage.'

He paused and tightened his grip on Lovedeep's wrist. 'Do you have courage?' he asked.

Nothing happened for a long time after that.

Ian opened a second can for himself. Lovedeep watched as he took a drink. Time had begun to move in such extraordinary slow motion that she was sure, at first, that the can would never reach his lips; and when it did, that it would never leave them. It did that too. The moment released a flood of thoughts. They all tumbled on top of her at once, as though a bookshelf had been pushed over and crashed down on her, with all its ideas and people and stories intact. He was the killer. She laughed inwardly. He was going to kill her. Was he? Yes, of course he was. That's what killers do. They kill people. She laughed inwardly at that too. Killers kill people. It was so true it was absurd. But here he was, waiting to kill. Nothing like this had ever happened to Lovedeep before. She had to laugh at that too. Of course it hadn't. If it had, she'd be dead. She thought suddenly of her mother, sitting at home. She would be watching cable at this hour. Her father would be complaining about her mother watching cable. Her mother always watched the same shows, and he always complained. Yet he watched the same shows and others besides. She had said this to him, so had Mom. He never listened. He could watch whatever he wanted, he paid the cable bill.

Ian's grip tightened and she realized she was crying.

'I won't scream,' she said suddenly. 'I won't make any noise.'

The words came out of her. She had no idea why, or whether she would scream or not. Ian's grip relaxed momentarily and she felt the soothing brush of his fingers across her sweat-moistened skin.

'It doesn't matter either way,' he said. 'Do whatever you want.'

What a flood of memories! She wanted to talk about all of them. She wanted to tell Ian. Perhaps he would understand, he would see her clearly, exactly as she was, and let her go, because how could you kill someone you saw clearly? She would tell him about the time when she was four, or was it five? Oh, it mattered! If she couldn't remember the age, how could she remember clearly. No, she was five. She knew it now. Walking down the street, lost, her parents disappeared, and an old man appearing out of nowhere and terrifying her with his old hands and his old face. The light of the afternoon seemed to jump away from him and left them both in a circle of darkness. That's what she remembered. That *circle*.

A first drunken kiss in a high school bathroom with Jeremy Drake who had not washed his hair in a month. She kissed him out of pity, terror, curiosity. Everything she did seemed to grow out of those three emotions, the primary colours painting her world. Except she could not remember the last thing she had done solely out of curiosity. Should she tell Ian about the icy arguments that reigned throughout her childhood, how they formed her, an only child, sitting as if on the periphery of a battle she had no part in except as spoils of victory?

Ian's pulse beat through his fingertips and against her wrist. She closed her eyes. She was only a year old when her father, laughing giddily, threw her up high into the air. Oh, it was like jumping over the moon! Up high, then down. Whoosh! He caught her with such confidence. Oh, how she loved that! Then up again, high into the spinning, beautiful air! To be held like that again by Papa!

Could she tell Ian that? Would it melt his heart?

But she wasn't a killer. How did she know who killed and why, and what stopped them? She opened her eyes. He had not moved. His head remained tilted back, staring at the ceiling.

'Should I put music on?' she said. Her voice was thin and weak.

'I don't like music.'

'What do you like?'

'I don't like things. I thought I did once. I had aspirations to liking things. I thought I could walk out the door, see the sky, and say to myself, That's a pretty sky. Or see a girl walking along, and say, That's a pretty girl. Or just walk, walk down the street, and say, How good it feels to walk down the street.'

His grip tightened again and Lovedeep stifled a scream.

After a minute, he relaxed the pressure and continued, 'I'd say it, all those things, every one of them. Then one day, it hit me. Every word I said was a lie. I didn't feel one thing. Good, bad, ugly. I felt nothing. For years I'd been walking around lying to myself. Doesn't that make you sick? A man who spent his whole life lying to himself. What a miserable creature.'

'I think you're a good man,' Lovedeep said. 'A man who knows what he wants.'

He released her wrist and stood and pulled the camera from its case. It was a handheld digital with a fold-out viewfinder. His right arm was shaking violently.

'Does it always do that?' she asked.

'Since I was a kid.'

'I'm sorry.'

He nodded. 'This helps.'

She pointed to the camera.

'Do you have the others on there?' she said.

'The last.'

'Can I see?'

'I'll plug it into your TV. The picture'll be better.'

It occurred to Lovedeep that she had grown calm, and she did not know why. As Ian fussed with various cords and connections, she asked herself if this was what her whole life had been building toward, her test, her proof, her vindication? She would look death in the eye, she would not flinch.

'Here it is,' he said.

They watched in silence. The woman's face did look peaceful. She remembered it from the glimpse at the happy hour bar. And beautiful. Ian was right. It was as if the dead woman had witnessed a final secret. A blissful peace wrapped her features and Lovedeep hoped she would look as pretty, as rested, as *completed*, as this woman did in the video. But what had she ever done? She felt suddenly small and stupid, that her life was coming to an end and this was all, this wasteland of an apartment, this unmarried life, childless. Who had she ever cared for? What accomplishments did she leave behind, what unspoken mercies done for strangers? She remembered the instructor at the class that evening. Lovedeep suddenly wanted to go to India, she wanted to go to many places. Maybe she could make a deal. Travel six months, a year, come back to this very room, exactly as they were here. She wanted so much to leave something behind. But no. All hope left her. If she had never done anything, how could she expect to now. Ian, she knew, understood this.

Lovedeep was crying again. She wiped her eyes with the sleeve of her blouse.

'Time to take off the belt,' Ian said.

She stood shakily and untied the belt from her waist and held it out, feeling stupid, her knees weak, thinking how surprisingly gentle he was, that such a gentle man could not be about to kill her. But that if he did, and she was sure he was going to, for why else was he here, she would die at the hands of a gentle man, this man.

'You don't hate me, do you?' she said.

He was tearing open the plastic wrapping of a new videotape.

'Yes,' he said. 'I do.' He added, softly, 'Don't take it personally, it's women.'

He pressed a button on the camera and the old tape popped out. He replaced it with the blank one.

'I like using a fresh tape. Nowadays these tapes go on for hours. I only use a few minutes. It's a waste. I'm just no good at breaking habits.' He turned to her, eyes blank. 'I'll use the belt. I haven't done that in a while. The last two I used my hands.'

She liked the idea of his hands. It was intimate. Perhaps he would change his mind at the last moment.

'I'll be on cable,' Lovedeep said, then she let out a low-pitched scream and dropped to her knees.

He stared down at her with disinterest. 'I thought you were going to be a good girl.'

Lovedeep pressed her fingers into her mouth.

'I'm sorry. I will. I'll be a good girl. Promise.'

He held out a hand. 'Here.' He helped Lovedeep to her feet. He wrapped an arm around her waist and rested his face against hers. She could feel the hard brush of his stubble and smell him. He smelt of glue and something burning, a fire, old ashes.

'Don't worry,' he said. 'It'll be over quickly. You've been good so far.' He added, 'Can I tell you a secret?'

'Yes?'

'You've been the best. I've never had one like you. I couldn't dream of a better one. Your parents raised you well. It's a shame.'

'Really?'

'I promise. I can't wait to see your face. There's nothing like it in the world.'

'I wish I could see it.'

Ian pulled away and handed Lovedeep a beer. 'Last one,' he said. It was with great difficulty that she popped the can open. Her fingers felt like water. This time, it didn't taste so bad. She almost liked it. Maybe she was finally developing a taste for cheap beer.

'My hand is shaking,' she said. 'Like yours.'

'That's normal.'

He reached forward and draped the belt around Lovedeep's shoulders, then pulled one end all the way through the broad silver buckle until she found it difficult to breathe. The buckle caused her head to be forced back. To watch what Ian was doing, she had to strain her eyes as if looking sharply downward.

'Don't worry,' he said. 'I'm just getting ready.'

Lovedeep dropped the beer at her feet. She bent her body forward to watch the liquid hiccup out through the narrow opening. What a mess someone would find with the spilled beer staining the carpet next to her body.

'Did something happen to you?' Lovedeep's voice seeped out in tortured gasps. 'When you were little?'

Ian was cueing the video camera.

'I don't remember much. I had a mom. I guess I got beat up, I was a weak kid. I watched an old house burn. People were in it. Girls mostly. I did some rotten things. I'm not a saint.'

He placed the camera on the table and turned to Lovedeep and without warning, violently yanked at the free end of the belt and pulled it tight. Her head flew forward and she let out a strangled cry.

'I've never done an Indian before,' he said. His face was pressed up against hers. 'I think I like it.' He grinned. 'I lied. There are some things I like.' He pulled the belt tighter. 'People always told me Indian girls were good. What did I know? I don't go in for spiritual bullshit. Maybe I'm finally seeing the light.'

As Lovedeep crumpled to the floor, the last thing she saw was Ian's arm. It had stopped shaking.

Sanskrit

It is past seven when Anu hears the key in the door and a moment later, Hari's voice calling from the hall.

'Don't move,' she shouts. 'Don't go anywhere.'

'I need to piss. I'm desperate.'

She appears, holding a camera in one hand and a silver cone party hat in the other. The camera is disposable. She picked it up in the city, when she left work early, afraid she wouldn't find their camera at home. It makes no difference that she is the one who puts everything away, she can never find anything.

'Put this on,' she says.

Hari waves the hat away with an arm draped with a black overcoat. He drops his briefcase against the wall.

'I need to piss.'

'Darling.'

'Okay, make it quick.'

She straps the hat onto Hari's head and kisses him on the cheek.

'Happy birthday.'

She steps back and snaps a photo.

'Did the flash go?'

'Yes,' Hari says. 'Now …'

'It didn't.'

'Fine, it didn't. You had your chance.'

Hari walks past her, leaving the coat in her arms.

'What happened?' she calls after him.

'Bomb at Grand Central.'

'An explosion?'

'No, just a scare. A bomb scare. The place was evacuated.'

The downstairs bathroom door opens but doesn't close. Hari enjoys taking a piss with the door open. It's more intimate, more married somehow. Anu thinks it gross. She can hear him pissing.

'Whisky soda?' she asks.

'Sure.'

He is leaning against the doorjamb leading to the kitchen, his fly undone, the party hat still on his head.

'I needed that.'

'Here,' handing him the whisky.

'Kiss me,' he says.

'I have to change.'

'Change?'

'You didn't think I'd dress like this.'

'How do you dress?'

'You'll see.'

Hari takes a long drink and nods to the bottle. Anu refills his glass.

'And?' he asks.

'It's a surprise.'

He winks theatrically. 'I picked up something too.'

'What?'

Hari reaches into his inside jacket pocket and produces a rolled-up Ziploc bag. Raising it over his head, he unfurls it with a snap of his wrist.

'Pot,' Anu says, bringing her face up to the bag. 'That's cool.'

'Bolinas razorback. This is serious shit. Organic, hydroponic, the works.'

'Roll one, will you? I'm going to change. There's a couple burgers in the bag.'

Hari spots the Wendy's bag on the counter.

'Birthday dinner?'

'Go ahead, stuff your face. I'll be in the bedroom. No peeking.'

He takes a framed photograph down from the wall, an enlarged black and white showing his father as a young man standing in a lush Ludhiana garden, wearing a suit and tie and holding an umbrella, both hands on the handle, tip pressed into the ground, like Steed in *The Avengers*. He sets the photograph on the coffee table, taps out a portion of pot onto the glass, and begins to press it through his fingers, sorting out the stems. He pulls a packet of papers from his pocket, Big Bambi, purchased at the corner store on West 40th, where he picks up his coffee mornings.

The phone rings as he finishes rolling the joint. He checks the caller ID before answering.

'Jack,' he says.

'I don't feel motion, Harry, I don't feel anything moving. Are things in motion? Are we moving?'

'There is motion, Jack. There is motion on several fronts.'

'I am walking inside a miasma. I am walking round and round in a vast circle. I'm going to walk and discover my own footprints one day. That's how I feel.'

'It's going around.'

'You're a funny man. You should do stand-up.'

'We're making an assault, Jack. Planning stages, there are ground forces, there are recon teams. We have radar up and active, we have infiltration. We are on the verge of initiating first contact. Penetration is imminent.'

'Henderson?'

'Hawthorne.'

'What are you doing right now?'

'I rolled a joint. I hope that's not against policy?'

Hari lights the joint and takes a puff.

'Tell me, Harry. You don't have kids?'

'You don't know?'

'I know. I want to hear it from you.'

'No, Jack, no kids.'

'What does that mean?'

'Jack?'

'What does it mean not to have kids?'

'It's quiet. That's what it means. It's quiet and I get to fuck my wife on my birthday.'

'That's why I was calling. I wanted to wish you a happy birthday. I almost forgot. It's amazing. I think I am losing my way.'

'Thanks.'

'Do you have a copy of *Cosmo*? If not, then *Marie Claire*. One of those.'

'The magazines?'

'Wives subscribe. It's a basic principle.'

Anu does, he knows, and as he turns to search the shelf below the side table, he is stopped by what he sees resting before the framed photograph of Anu's mother. It is a penis. Nothing more and nothing less. It is dark, flaccid, sitting atop a pair of balls. He reaches out a finger and pokes it. It feels soft, just like his.

He pulls the stack of magazines out from the lower shelf and sorts through them on his lap.

'Harry? Do you have the magazine?'

'Hold on, I've got a situation.'

'What kind of situation are we talking?'

'Nothing for you to worry about. I have *Cosmo* here.'

'Good. Page 158. I need you to turn to page 158.'

As he turns the pages, he lays the rubber penis on his knee and stares at it, the dark, ribbed flesh, the curl of the shaft, the uncircumcised foreskin. It's not hard like a dildo. It's soft and it looks like the real thing, except the base is cleanly sliced and MADE IN INDIA stamped into it. It shivers when he moves his knee, it rocks back and forth when he raises and lowers it. It is almost alive and he has to fight an impulse to reach out and stroke it.

'There's an ad,' Hari says, 'and an article about that actress from Idaho.'

'Put your face in the ad.'

'The perfume ad.'

'Yes. Put your face in it. Close your eyes. Then open the flap and breathe in. Inhale. I want you to inhale deeply before you open your eyes.'

The perfume is called Homicide.

'I smell it.'

'Good. Now open your eyes.'

Hari sees a naked woman, maybe sixteen, full, long blonde hair, eyes shut, a look of ecstasy on her face. He takes another toke.

'She's fuckable,' Hari says. 'Uber fuckable.'

'She is Willomena von Stettin-Coburg, original euro-trash royalty.'

'Nice. What are we talking about, Jack?'

'Your birthday present. We have a company discount. One grand. For one grand she will give you a blow job. She doesn't fuck. No one. I've looked into it.'

'Jesus.'

'It's one hell of a blowjob. Top-notch production values, five-piece band, singer, professional lighting. The full-on razzmatazz. You'll never look back. She'll change your life, you'll be a spoiled man.'

'She is good?'

'Better. Have Peggy set you up. I'll call you later.'

She lies snaking across the perfumed fold, on her side, head thrown back, breasts vivid, even a shadow of pubic hair visible. Hari thinks about her mouth, her mouth around his dick.

He hears Anu let out a cry.

'Honey?'

There is a long silence and he returns his attention to the woman in the magazine.

'Honey?' he calls again.

'Nothing,' she says from somewhere in the house. 'I hate India.'

'What is it?' He lifts the penis to his face. He holds it in the palm of his hand, level with his eyes, and shakes it, watching it wobble. A molded jelly dessert, he thinks.

'They don't teach you how to wear one!'

'Wear what?' He brings the penis to his mouth, holds it up against his lips, slides his tongue along the rubber foreskin. How do women do it?

'Hold on.'

He stands and fits the rubber penis into his open fly and walks to the bedroom door. With every step it shivers like the real thing.

'Honey?' he knocks.

'Soon.'

He waits, a hand idly playing with his second cock.

Anu appears in the half-light of the hall.

'Get on your knees,' he orders softly.

'What?'

'Get on your knees and suck my dick.'

She is dressed in a silver and blue sari, awkwardly, nothing right about it but he can't say what fails, what is wrong. Before he can look closely, she is on her knees, her mouth around the rubber cock.

She pulls back, the penis in her mouth, and lets it fall. 'Oh god,' she cries, drops with her back against the wall. 'Oh god.' She looks up, laughing, at Hari. 'I hate you. I thought it was ...'

'Yes,' he says, getting down on his knees. She is beautiful in the half-light of the hall, in the disordered sari, the surprised grin on her face.

'Kiss me,' he says.

'Later.'

'What's going on?'

'I had to staple it. Staple it everywhere.' She is almost in tears. 'Look at me. I'm a disaster. I don't know how, I don't know anything. I'm supposed to be an Indian woman. This is what I'm going to teach my daughter. God, I hate myself. I can't do anything. Not anything.'

'Here,' handing her the joint.

She takes a long toke, hands it back, and picks up the rubber penis. 'I couldn't resist. I saw it there today and I had to. You understand?'

'I'm flying,' Hari says. 'That's all. I'm flying.'

'You are. I want to know. Tell me everything.'

'I don't know what it means. I can't feel my arms.'

'Yes?'

'No, I mean, I feel my arms. It's like.'

'Yes?'

'I feel my arms for the first time. It's like I never felt my arms before. These are my arms. I feel them.'

'That's wild.'

'They're so there. On my body. Like they're real. Like they're real and they're real at the same time. Like I think they're there and there they are. They are there.'

'You have arms.'

'I have arms.'

The telephone rings. The landline. He jumps but she stops him with a hand on his shoulder.

'I'll get it,' Anu says, taking short, unsteady steps, her legs caught in the tightly wound sari. She looks Japanese, a geisha in a kimono, gingerly carrying the rubber penis.

'Hello, Mom,' she says.

'What time is it over there?'

'What?'

'The time. What time where you are?'

'The same time as you.'

'Oh.' Her mother lets out a laugh. 'I was talking to India. I got confused.'

'I'm busy, Mom. Is there something?'

'Nothing. Well, yes, something.'

'What?'

'Oh, nothing. Maybe another time.'

'Okay. It's Hari's birthday. Do you want to say hello?'

'No, you tell him happy birthday.'

'I will.'

'Wait. Just one thing. Where does he carry his cell phone?'

'What?'

'Where does he keep it? In his jacket pocket or his trouser pocket?'

'I don't know. Why do you want to know?'

'I'm worried. You've been married for four years, and nothing. No baby.'

'Yes, Mom, we're waiting. We're taking precautions. When the time's right. We've talked, I've told you this.'

'Tell him to be careful. Not to keep his phone in his pants. I read today it damages the male sperm. The radioactivity. It makes monster children.'

'Mom? Hold on.'

'What?'

'Another call.' She clicks on the other line. 'Hello?'

'Anu? Is that you, Anu?'

'Mom? Hold on, I'm on the other line.' She clicks back. 'Mom?'

'The sperm, Anu, Hari's sperm.'

'I've got to go. It's Hari's mother.'

'But I'm your mother.'

'She's Hari's mother.'

'I'm Hari's mother.'

'She's my mother.'

'I'll call you later. Don't forget, Hari's sperm.'

'Hello? Hold on, I'll get Hari.'

She lowers the phone and places a hand over the mouthpiece. 'Your mom,' she calls. He appears from the kitchen, holding a whisky, and makes a puking motion, then strangles himself with one hand and feints a fall to the floor.

'I think he must be in the bathroom. I'll tell him to call you.'

'What time is it there?'

'Oh, just past eight.'

'It's five o'clock here. The sun is out. It's raining.'

'It's setting here.'

'Nothing like California. You don't know what you're missing.'

'Maybe one day.'

'What are you doing? A party?'

'No, nothing special. Dinner, maybe a movie later. We're boring people these days.'

'No, not yet. You don't have children yet. Then you'll be boring.'

'I know.'

'Well ...?'

'What?' She looks across at Hari and rolls her eyes. He is standing in the kitchen doorway, grinning, places the drink on the counter, and mimes a full blast from a machine gun, mouth silently screaming, 'Rat-a-tat-a-tat-tat!'

'What is it you two get up to? Just dinner, just a movie? Hari's father is waiting, I am waiting. We're in California and we're waiting. Everyone is waiting.'

'Yes, yes. The whole world is waiting. Look, Mom, I'll have Hari call you when he's down.'

'Oh no, don't trouble him, not on his birthday. Tell him I telephoned. He'll be happy to hear his mother telephoned.'

'Homicide?' she says after she places the phone down, the magazine open on the table before her.

He sings. 'Psycho killer, qu'est-ce que c'est?'

'Bedroom,' she says. 'Now.'

Hari's cell phone rings.

'Leave it,' she says.

'I can't,' he says. 'It's Jack.'

'Just one thing,' Jack says. 'A word of advice.'

Anu walks into the kitchen and finds the joint. She climbs up onto the counter, still holding the rubber penis, and places it in her mouth. Hari watches her. He can see the staples, they are everywhere, lines of them along each fold, each twist of the sari. The whole thing is a mess, nothing like how a sari should look. Each time she moves, a new line of staples catches the light. There must be hundreds of them.

'Sure,' Hari says.

'Change your name. Shorten it,' Jack says.

'This is about Hawthorne?'

'This is personal. Think of it as a birthday bonus.'

'What do you mean?'

'My name is Jack. Understand? One word, one syllable. That's American. Your name is Harry. Two syllables. Good men died to be free of that second syllable.'

'I'm Indian, Jack. Hari is an Indian name.'

'Chinese, European, same difference. We're talking American. We're speaking to each other in a country where no one gives a damn about that second syllable. Bob, Bill, Mike, John, Fred, Art, Jake, Zack. These are American names. I want you to choose one.'

'Now?'

'When you feel like it. There's no pressure. Myself, I see you as Dick. Jack and Dick. Dick and Jack. With a name like that, we might be partners one day.'

'Are you making an offer?'

'This is an opening. This is a potential first step. I like what you're doing with Hawthorne.'

'Thanks.'

'I'll call you later.'

'Dick,' Hari says. 'What do you think of Dick?'

'I love it,' Anu says, pulling the rubber penis out of her mouth.

'I'm flying,' Hari says. 'I'm on the moon.'

His shirt is off and both his wrists are handcuffed to the bed frame. The handcuffs are padded with felt. Anu is working on tying his legs when the doorbell rings.

'Fuck,' she says.

'Ignore it.'

'No. I'll see. It might be someone.'

She rises, confused. He watches her disappear in a constricted rustle of silk and staple.

'Mrs Kastenbaum,' she says, realizing she is talking loud, trying to hide how stoned she is.

Mrs Kastenbaum stands in the doorway, a short, plump woman with white hair, holding a potted plant.

'It's a money plant,' she says. 'I thought. It brings you money.'

'That's kind, that's very kind. Thank you. How did you know?'

'Know what?'

'Hari's birthday.'

'Oh my goodness, no. What a coincidence. Is he okay? Did he make it home without a problem? I'm terrified just thinking about it. I'm still shaking.'

'Did something happen?'

'Nerve gas. They released nerve gas, I'm sure of it.'

'What are you talking about?'

'At Grand Central Station, underground. People are dying, they will die. They will choke on their bathroom floors. I know it.'

'It was a bomb scare.'

Mrs Kastenbaum blinks, looks at Anu closely, as if her eyes have been closed this whole time, as if suddenly, after many decades of being blind, she has been miraculously given sight again.

'It's a sari,' Anu says.

'You stapled it.'

'I know . . . I just—'

'I've never seen anything so . . . so . . .'

'Yes?'

'You dress like this every night?'

'Well, not …'

'You must be deeply rooted people.'

'It's just …'

'I thought of you two as a modern couple, you know, drugs, parties, electrical devices, that sort of thing. Who knows? Adultery?'

'Yes.'

'It is so rare, people who take the past seriously, people who respect their parents, their mothers. No one respects their mother anymore.'

'Yes.'

'Will you say something for me?'

'I don't understand.'

'In your language.'

'In English?'

'English?'

'I'm speaking it now.'

'No. In Sanskrit.'

'Sanskrit?'

'I've always wanted someone to say something to me in Sanskrit. I've never had the courage to ask.'

'No one speaks it.'

'No one?'

'It's for the gods.'

'Oh—'

Mrs Kastenbaum turns to leave and stops. 'People are dying,' she says.

Hari's cell starts to ring the moment Anu enters the bedroom.

'Quick,' he says. 'See if it's Jack.'

'It's Jack.'

'Hold it to my face.'

She answers the phone. 'Here he is, Jack,' she says.

'Jack?'

'I'll make this quick,' Jack says. 'This is about Hawthorne.'

'Go ahead.'

Anu hovers over him, lit by candles on all sides, her hair falling down about his eyes. He is watching her the whole time he talks to Jack, her eyes, mouth, lips. Who is she? How did they marry? How did they meet? The past is oblivion.

'Stick him like a pig,' Jack says. 'Stick him and stick him hard. Up the ass. Do you hear me?'

'I hear you.'

'You'll get one chance with Hawthorne, maybe not even that. He has his mouth wrapped around Keppenmeyer's dick. He's sucking hard. You need to be aware of this. I want you to stick him in the ass and make the shit scream. I want to see shit flying out of his mouth. Is your dick big enough for that?'

'My dick's big enough.'

There is a long silence.

'Jack?'

'I am in the abyss, Harry. I am staring into the abyss. I am falling. It's a very long way down.'

'You'll be fine, Jack. We all will.'

'I like your attitude. It's a great reassurance. I don't know if it's enough. There are things you don't know.'

'Yes, Jack.'

'Remember. Hawthorne takes it in the ass. I'll call you later.'

Anu shuts the phone and drops it on the bed.

She says, 'One of these days, you're going to have to tell me what you do for that man.'

She is watching, she is looking at his face, at the shadows, the play of light created by the candles.

'My feet,' he says. 'Tie my feet.'

'Wait. I want to say something, I want ...'

She loses the thread. For a moment she saw something, something vital and deep in his eyes, about herself, about him, about the two of them together. In a flash it is gone.

'I'm losing my mind,' she says.

'Not you too.'

'No, just ...'

'Yes?'

'Mrs Kastenbaum thinks we speak Sanskrit.'

'We don't?'

'No one does, darling.'

'Not even when we were little?'

'Don't ask me, I'm flying.'

'Tie my legs.'

'Which ones are your legs?' She falls forward onto his chest. 'Did you eat both the burgers?'

She licks his neck, up, across, to his ear.

'Tie me till it hurts,' he says.

She raises herself on her elbows and looks at him hard.

'Pig,' she says.

His cell phone rings.

'Hey Jack,' Anu says. 'Long time no speakee.'

'Annie,' Jack says. 'I need Harry.'

'He's all tied up.'

'Darling,' Hari says. 'Hold it to my face.'

She shakes her head. 'Fuck you.'

'Jack,' he shouts. 'Ignore her. She's talking to me.'

She shuts the phone and drops it on the floor.

'Cunt,' he says.

'Prick,' she says.

'Fuck me,' he says.

'No,' she says.

The phone rings again.

'Hold it this time.'

She sticks her tongue out and holds the phone to his ear.

'Harry, that you?'

'I'm right here, Jack.'

'I'm having a crisis, Harry. You're the only man I can talk to about these things. The two of us share a natural affinity for order and a well-regulated life. We are blood brothers, we are kin of a higher order. I look upon you as my spiritual body double. I'll hire you to impersonate me in heaven one day.'

Anu bites his nipple and he stops himself from letting out a cry.

'Do you mind if I call you Dick?'

'Go ahead.'

'Okay, Dick. Don't you like the sound of that?'

'Sure. What's on your mind?'

'Could it be that I am not who I am?'

'What are you getting at?'

'Those movies, you must have seen them when you were a kid. Body snatchers, aliens with the power of mind control, top secret government experiments. Maybe I am an alien in my own body, maybe I am someone else entirely. I might be sitting right now in a room in Arlington, Virginia, and here is my body, walking around an office in midtown.'

'That's the movies. In the movies, no one is who he is.'

Anu is running her tongue along his throat, his chin, a foot playing over his crotch.

'That's an interesting idea, Dick. I'm impressed. But what about the one where Heston plays Van Gogh? Is he Heston? Is he the painter? Who is he, if he's not one or the other?'

'Jack?'

'Yes, Dick?'

'What are we talking about?'

'I'll tell you a story, Dick. I once put a loaded pistol up my first wife's cunt. It was my grandfather's gun. He carried it in the Great War. Then it was my father's. He carried in the Second World War. Then it was mine. I pushed it up my wife's cunt one night and I told her I was going to kill her if she refused to give me a divorce.'

'What happened?'

'She said no. I pulled the trigger. I'm not kidding. The gun was loaded and I pulled the trigger. I don't know why I'm telling you this, Dick. I've never told anyone, not even my lawyer.'

'Did she die, Jack? Did you kill her?'

Jack says nothing.

'Jack?'

Anu releases one of Hari's wrists and brings his hand to the phone. She raises herself, first on all fours, straddling his body like a cat, the sari falling from her figure and across his chest, then is free of him.

'That's the beautiful thing,' Jack says finally. 'In all those years, that gun never once misfired. That was the one time it did. I tell you, Dick, I had the best sex of my life that night, the very best. It remains unequalled.'

Hari shoots her a look of alarm and she puts a finger to her lips and tiptoes out.

In the kitchen, all the way at the back of the cupboard over the microwave, she finds her stash of Dunhills. Not even Hari knows about them. She pulls out a pack and matches and takes them outside, to the concrete porch, and sits down in the cool night air. She can hear Hari calling after her.

She lights a cigarette, inhales deeply. It has been six months since she last smoked. The tobacco tastes stale, glorious. Despite the high, it goes straight to her head.

Across the street, she sees Mrs Kastenbaum at her kitchen window, face framed by bright yellow ruffled curtains. Her face is deformed and ugly and frightening. Her eyes are enormous insect eyes, staring through the window glass. It takes Anu a moment to realize Mrs Kastenbaum is holding a pair of binoculars to her face. The old woman lowers them and raises an arm and waves.

The Bolinas razorback kicks in. It is sudden, like the drug has been puttering her along in second gear for miles and with one punch of the pedal shoots her up to fifth.

Everything transforms.

She looks up at the few stars, the sky is burning, it is on fire, stars are falling from the heavens. She is melting into the concrete. Everything is molten, the street, the houses, the whole city is a river of flames. She can see Mrs Kastenbaum. The two large insect eyes are at her face again, hovering in the kitchen.

Anu wants to say something. She wants to tell Mrs Kastenbaum something desperately important. She tries. She opens her mouth. She forms the words. Nothing comes out. The words are stuck in her throat. They are not even words, they are sounds, the sounds people made before they could say anything.

She stubs the cigarette out, lights another. Inhales. The world is fire, she thinks, and tries to make a sound and fails. When she looks up, Mrs Kastenbaum is gone.

Hero of the Nation

THE FIRST TIME I MET PAPA WAS WHEN HE CAME TO LIVE WITH US IN the spring, when things were growing. In an uncharacteristic mood of celebration, Mom planted a row of colourful flowers in the front yard along both sides of the driveway. Daisies and buttercups and even a rose bush. A week later, I was the one who found Papa peeing on the flowers. His ancient penis was gripped between his fingers, his lower lip curled over his upper. He looked like a garden gnome, except that he was out-sized and he had, strangely, a working dick.

'The bastard,' Mom said, shooing him back into the house. 'I'll never do another thing for him.'

I clipped two roses for Papa and left them on his pillow. I was on his side, I decided.

Papa was Dad's father, a man in his seventies who had spent his life in the military in India. I asked Dad how many wars he'd fought in and Dad said, 'Don't be an idiot. Girls don't need to know about things like that.'

I'd heard stories, mostly in whispers, of my soldier grandfather, far away in India. The few photographs of him hanging in the house fascinated me. There he was, stern and handsome in his turban and his neat beard and proper military moustache, decked out in his crisp uniform. I dreamt of his adventures on the front lines of wars I knew nothing about, and in my mind all his battles took place on the slopes of high snow-covered mountains. He would struggle for hours through the mist, carrying an enormous pack, only to suddenly confront the enemy directly in the zero-visibility of a blizzard. He always won these hand-to-hand fights, and he always slit the throat of his enemy with his bayonet so that blood splattered gregarious and red across the white snow.

It was a shock to meet him finally, bent, his eyes filmy with age, his figure straining against collapse.

'The old fool has come here to die,' Dad mused when he arrived. It was Papa's first time in the US. Dad invited him every year and every year Papa refused. Dad said Papa was stubborn, that he never liked the idea of his children moving away. Now he came because there was nowhere else for him to go. The old man had lost his strength, while his mind, Dad said, was going. He'd also lost the power of speech. When he tried to talk, he moved his jaw up and down and a painful rattle emerged. Dad refused to tell me what happened. I searched Papa's old neck for a gunshot wound but found only a thin, inconclusive scar. At night I'd lie awake thinking of him, this one-time hero of his nation, reduced to wordless sorrow and a life little better than that of an animal chained and dying in its pen.

My brother Johnny said they cut your tongue out when you retired from the army, that way you couldn't reveal state secrets. I knew that's not what happened, for there was Papa's tongue, a curled sentry greeting all when he opened and shut his great mouth. Johnny had another name, an Indian name, but no one used it. I hated mine, Ruby, short for Rupinder. Every week I secretly changed it. One week it was Gloriana, the next it was Xerxes. I'd exhausted the standards: Ashley, Heather, Mary, Juliet. I was worried one day I'd run out and have to become a boy to find a name that suited me.

A month after Papa arrived I learned why he couldn't speak. He was a lifelong smoker, contracted throat cancer, and the operation that saved his life cost him the power of speech. I learned this by listening in on a phone conversation Dad was having with his sister in Phoenix.

'Papa used to smoke,' I said to Dad that evening.

Mom looked at me across the dinner table. 'Don't talk like that in front of your father.'

Papa was sitting to one side of the dinner table, in his own special chair, a big baby chair, a bib printed with pastel-coloured unicorns around his neck and a small table at his elbow.

'What did I say?'

'You know exactly what you said,' Mom said.

I did know. Sikhs don't smoke. It's one of the rules. Like Sikhs don't cut their hair and Sikhs don't drink. Smoking one cigarette is almost as bad as killing someone.

'Who told you he smoked?' Dad said.

'No one. I thought that was why he couldn't speak.'

Papa grinned at me each time I spoke.

'He was in the army,' Dad said. 'Things happen in the army.'

I nodded, 'Oh,' and went on eating.

Johnny jabbed me in the ribs. 'Shit for brains,' he whispered.

Suddenly Mom made a face.

'Oh god,' she said.

A thin stream of urine was dripping from along the edge of Papa's chair and he grinned broadly at all of us now.

'He's your father,' Mom said to Dad. 'You clean it up.'

The next day, Mom bought twelve boxes of Depend undergarments. I watched as she stacked one after the other in the cupboard under the stairs. I could tell she was angry. She punched each one into the wall, like she was shoring it up against a flood.

'Can I try one on?' I said.

She ignored me and punched the last box into place, slapped her hands together, and turned and bumped straight into me as she was walking out.

'You,' she said.

'Can I try one on?' I said again.

'They're not for you.' She slammed the cupboard door.

'How many people did Papa kill?' I said.

'What?'

'Papa? How many did he kill?'

Mom considered me with distaste. 'You and your questions. Is that all they teach you at that school?'

She turned away and walked into the kitchen. It was time for Papa's lunch.

That school was a special needs school. I had started there two years ago. I talked too much, asked too many questions, couldn't concentrate; the doctors said one thing, gave me pills; Mom said I needed discipline; Dad looked around for the right kind of school. We were all girls. Half the universe was erased the moment we walked through the gates. It didn't bother me, I liked the school well enough, except we learned little and were left mostly to ourselves, to taunt and tease and make up stories as we liked, and during recess we would wander in circles through the courtyard and pretend we all had futures which the bright ones amongst us knew we didn't.

When Mom was gone, I climbed into the cupboard, switched the light on, a dim, bare bulb, and closed the door behind me. I opened the first box, pulled out one of the adult diapers and held it to the light. It looked exactly like a baby's disposable diaper, only larger, as though it was made for a mutant, the kind they used to make bad movies about in the fifties. Two blue buttons were sewn to the front to hook it up with. I pressed it to my face. It smelled of plastic and cardboard and glue.

I pulled my jeans off and my panties down and slipped into the diaper and buttoned it up. I felt anxious and excited as I stood there, hunched over because of the low ceiling. The plastic felt warm against my skin. I dug in my jeans on the floor, produced a pack of cigarettes, Kools, and a book of matches. I tapped one out against my wrist, placed it in my mouth, and lit it. I stood there for a minute smoking, thinking something should happen, something magical and strange. I should instantly be transported into another dimension where the rules of the universe were reversed, where black was white, where up was down, where the world I knew had never so much as been imagined.

Because there I was, standing in the closet, smoking, wearing an adult diaper.

But nothing happened, so what could I do but stub the cigarette out, pull the diaper off, and replace it in the box?

Johnny was in the backyard, playing on the swing. Papa sat in the shade in a deck chair, his pink turban lopsided on his head. I could tell he was watching Johnny from the way his head moved back and forth with the motion of the swing.

I found Mom in the kitchen. She was chopping chicken with a cleaver.

'Can I put the diaper on Papa now?' I said.

'Don't be silly.'

'It's for training.'

'Training?'

'I'm planning to be a nurse.'

Mom looked at me with concern. She always did when I voiced any ambition.

She shook her head. 'I want your father to do it.'

I was leaving when Mom said, 'What's that smell?'

'What smell?'

'Come here.'

She pushed her nose into my hair. My heart began to explode in my chest.

'New shampoo?' she said.

'Yes,' I said. 'Peppermint. Like gum.'

Dad appeared late at dinner that night, one arm around

Papa, whom he helped down the stairs. When Papa was settled in his special chair, Dad poured himself a large whisky, no ice, and drank it in a single toss. He poured himself a second before joining us at the table.

No one spoke out loud. Only Johnny and me whispered almost silently to each other.

'Fuckwad,' Johnny said.

'Butt plug,' I said.

My name that night was Cassiopeia.

Later, I heard Dad on the phone.

'I hate him,' he said.

I was listening in on the extension downstairs as he talked to his sister. 'If I could . . .'

'Yes?' she said.

'I would.'

'What?'

'I don't have the guts.'

'He's an old man,' she said. 'He's our father.'

'I know.'

'I hate him as much as you do,' she said. 'More.'

'Yes?'

'I couldn't. Not ever.'

'I know.'

'You won't do anything?'

'I'm a coward,' Dad said.

I stopped listening when he said that. I hate cowards. I returned the phone loudly into the cradle and walked up the stairs to my room and banged my door shut.

Soon after, I heard footsteps outside my door. I knew it

was Dad, I recognized the way he walked. I could sense him standing there, holding a hand up as if to knock. He stood there for about a minute before I heard the steps move away.

From that day on, when Dad called his sister, he used a cell phone.

I cut school at lunch and returned home to an empty house. I thought I'd watch the afternoon movie. I shouted up and down the stairs. 'Mom, Papa.' No one. Maybe Mom had taken Papa out. I walked upstairs, excited by the freedom. I could hardly remember a time when I had the house entirely to myself. I stripped down to my underwear, slipped the pack of Kools into the elastic of my panties, lit a smoke, and began dancing along the hall.

First into Johnny's room, then Mom and Dad's, finally into the spare bedroom, where Papa slept.

I waltzed into Papa's bathroom. 'My name is Andromeda,' I sang.

He was lying on his back on the floor, pants around his ankles, arms waving weakly. His turban was knocked off his head and the room smelled foul, of old man urine and faeces.

'Papa?' I said. 'What happened?'

His eyes widened at my nudity and he threw a hand forward, attempting and failing, with an unsteady gesture, to block his view.

'It's okay, Papa,' I said. 'It's only me.'

I felt oddly brave standing there, like a soldier marching into battle. Even if he wanted to, he wouldn't be able to tell anyone. Crouching on the tiles and over his knees, I reached forward across his body and took hold of his turban. My plan was to replace it on his head, but the moment I lifted it, I pulled back. I watched his mouth tense and his eyes open wide with longing as he followed the passage of the cigarette, and then, for a second, his skin brushed mine. It felt dry and cold and cracked. A rattle emerged and I sensed him convulse.

I raised the pink turban, settled back on my haunches, and instead of replacing it on his head, fitted it onto mine.

It was large for me and slipped down over one ear and partially covered my right eye. I tapped a second cigarette out against my wrist, lit it and took several puffs, then leaned forward and slipped the cigarette between his lips. This was what he wanted, what he had wanted all along. His face transformed. The sternness disappeared, replaced by a giddy look of surprise, and there he was, a child again.

He lay there, trembling and eyes closed, the cigarette in his mouth, and I watched as his hand found his penis and grabbed hold of it roughly. It only took him a second to come. A tiny stream of ejaculate spread from the tip of his penis down its length. His hand once again drifted to his side and his body flagged. Within a minute, he was asleep.

'Send him to your sister,' Mom said. 'You can't be expected to take all the responsibility for this— for this—!'

We were gathered at the dinner table, all of us in our regular chairs, even Papa was there, the unicorn bib, now covered in turmeric-coloured stains, tied inexpertly by Dad around his neck.

After Papa had fallen asleep that afternoon, I eased the cigarette out of his mouth and left him there, alone on the bathroom floor, hoping he would sleep until Mom returned.

I spent the afternoon walking along the edge of the highway, where the roar of tyres on blacktop drowned my thoughts. Mom did find him. His hand was resting where he'd left it. I could hear her from my room, shouting at Dad when she told him. 'He was doing *that*—in his own shit!' I took up a position at the railing where I could listen more easily. 'He always hated you,' Mom shouted, 'and now he's come here so he can hate you properly.' Dad was silent for a long minute and I crept down along the stairway, hoping to catch his words.

'I know,' he said finally in a soft, defeated voice.

'So—?' Mom said.

Dad walked to the sideboard and poured himself a drink.

'He can't hurt anyone now. He's an old man and he was never much of anything, even when he was young. He's come here to die. We should let him.'

I stole back up the stairs, full of remorse, for Dad, for Papa, for all of us, for our sad, cowardly family. I'd be the one with courage, I decided, I wouldn't flinch. My name that night was Hecate, three-headed goddess. Dog, snake and horse.

'I can't send him to my sister,' Dad said, responding to Mom's demand, as we sat there at dinner. 'She has a family.' Around us, at the table, we were surrounded on all sides by the great empty cavern of the house.

Johnny whispered as they talked. 'Douche bag,' he said.

'And you don't?' Mom said. 'You don't have a family?'

'I didn't mean it that way,' Dad said.

'What did he do?' I asked. Even though I knew what had happened, I wanted to hear the version they'd give me.

'Nothing,' Dad said.

'Asscrack,' Johnny whispered.

'Then what way did you mean it?' Mom said.

'You're twisting my words.'

'What did he *do*?' I said, louder this time.

'Shit licker,' Johnny whispered.

'Nothing!' Dad said, suddenly very loud. 'The old bastard never did a thing in his life!'

We all fell into a momentary silence. Even Johnny stopped whispering.

Papa took hold of his plate in one hand and with a wild grip held it high. His stare moved violently from Dad to me and back again. Finally, he let the plate fall and it crashed with a loud thud on the floor and shattered. Warm dal spilled out across the carpet.

Dad closed his eyes.

'I'll clean it up,' I offered.

Mom threw an arm out and gripped my wrist to stop me from jumping. 'No. I want your father to. This is his problem.'

'I'll do it after we eat,' Dad said.

'I just meant today, Dad,' I explained. 'Not before.'

'Oh—' Dad stood and poured himself another drink and returned to the table.

'But he *was* a soldier,' I said. 'That's something.'

'He wasn't even in the army. Not the real army. He was a mechanic. Or something. I don't know. He never told me.'

'That's still something,' I said.

Dad groaned. 'He never killed anyone. Not on the battlefield. He doesn't even know how to fire a gun.'

I watched Papa silently. His lower lip was curled in anger and now he looked at me, eyes filled with accusation.

'It's very simple,' Mom said. 'You pick up the telephone and you call your sister.'

'And say what?'

'He's your father too. That's what you say.'

'Cocksucker,' Johnny whispered.

'Nothing?' I said.

'What?' Dad said.

'He did nothing?'

'Yes. Except he got a medal once. I think. By accident. He saved someone by accident. He was very proud of it.'

'You tell her that he's her father too,' Mom said. 'You insist.'

'How?' I said.

'By accident,' Dad repeated.

'What kind of accident?'

'She won't go for it,' Dad said, responding to Mom. 'You know it and I know it. She won't go for it.'

'Then make her,' Mom said.

'Cunt rag,' Johnny whispered.

'She's a bitch,' Dad said. 'There's no way to make her do anything.'

'Bitch,' Johnny said, out loud this time.

'Johnny—!' Mom scolded.

'*What—?*' Johnny said.

'What kind of accident?' I said.

Dad turned to me. 'Does it matter?'

'Yes.'

'He was fixing a Jeep. Someone was under it. The Jeep fell and crushed the guy. He held the Jeep up while someone pulled him out.'

'With his own hands?'

'Yes. He was that strong once. I remember.'

'Are you going to call her or not?' Mom said.

'No,' Dad said.

'What kind of man are you?' Mom said.

Without warning, Papa formed a fist and began pounding the small table at his elbow. He raised his fist and brought it down and raised it and brought it down. All the while, he stared at me.

Mom shook her head. 'I hate him,' she cried. 'I hate all of you!'

She jumped up and raced out of the room.

Dad waited a minute before he stood, finished his drink, and approached Papa from behind. The old man was pounding the table. Dad took hold of the fist and held it, suspended in midair. I could see Dad struggling under Papa's dying strength. The old man's muscles strained through his shirt, dense and round, and the veins on his knuckles were thick and discoloured. Dad held fiercely on, his eyes shut, his mouth tight. When he released Papa's hand, there were tears in his eyes.

Everyone was asleep when I emerged that night and padded silently along the upstairs carpet. The warm summer night echoed with the din of crickets in the yard and once in Papa's room, I switched the bathroom light on and left the door ajar so that his body was illuminated by an elongated rectangle spreading toward him. Standing at the end of the bed, I pulled the blanket down and off him. He was wearing a pajama suit, a red checked flannel. It was one of Dad's.

'Papa . . .' I said. 'Papa?'

He didn't move. His breath came in short, staggered bursts, catching in his throat. Without his turban, thick strands of unruly hair spread across the pillow in a withered delta of white. He looked like an ancient, an old god finally at rest.

'I am Hecate,' I said. 'I am the three-headed one.'

I lit a cigarette and dropped the match onto the carpet and stood there, smoking. He stirred at that. His chest heaved into gradual life, his arms and legs, and his old eyes opened nervously, and finally his mouth, cracking apart like a rock roasted in the desert sun, searching for words he would never be able to utter.

I climbed onto the bed, moving slowly, and advanced gingerly along his legs until I was straddling his crotch. I leaned forward and began to unbutton his pajama top. His whole body tensed and he attempted to sit up. I pushed him back with a forceful nudge of my palm. His chest was a mass of hairs, a white forest, the skin veined and old and troubled. It moved up and down, not with any regular motion, but with a sort of stop-and-start, as though at every moment his body was making the decision between life and death.

'Don't worry, Papa,' I said. 'I'm here to help you.'

He was trying to say something, to move, to rise. I placed a finger over his mouth, then I brought my hand down to his chest, splaying it out across his sternum. I took the cigarette from my mouth and slipped it between his lips.

'Is this what you want?'

He puffed, coughed, puffed again, and for a moment he looked serene.

I could feel his penis through the pajamas, pushing against my thigh. It was small and hard, like a boy's. His old, startled eyes gave me a look of fear.

'There's nothing to worry about, Papa,' I said.

Confusion widened across his face, as if he was beginning to understand. Were we communicating, I wondered, in some realm beyond the seen? I inched forward, sliding myself onto his belly, then his chest. He raised his hands to stop me. His mouth was open, the cigarette burning, drooping over his chin. I reached for it, took a puff, and returned it. He produced a gurgling cry and then his hands dropped once again.

'It's okay,' I said. 'Everything is going to be okay now.'

The smoke curled up my belly and hung in the air in thin, dissipated strands.

He grinned suddenly, like a retarded dog, his eyes sparkled, and I could see the stubs of yellowed teeth and the wet, diseased gums wrapping his skull and jaw, and under it, under all of that, the skin, the muscle, the straining ligaments, the now almost useless organs, I caught a glimpse of myself in his expression, as if deep inside, we understood each other, we were each one of us a failed warrior.

That was the moment.

I took hold of his pillow and brought it down, suddenly and violently, onto his face. His body gave a start and I could feel the features of his face, angry and terrified, struggling through the heavy fabric. His hands flew up and crashed against my chest and almost knocked me flying. Mustering my strength, I held his head locked in place while a faint choking scream emerged, and once again he bucked, his whole body rocking now. My eyes were shut, determined, while under me it was as if I had stuck a harpoon into a sea monster and was tumbling, lost, through the waves. He roiled under my arms, brought his hands to my thighs and dug his nails into my flesh. I choked back a scream. It was a long minute before I felt his hands slacken, the nails pull out, and his arms subside and eventually collapse. His strength deserted him and his chest sagged and the hard, maddening force of his neck finally relented and died.

I waited before I raised the pillow and climbed free and looked down at him. The cigarette was crushed, lying against his cheek. His eyes were shut and it was impossible to tell if he was breathing. A film of sweat covered his face. Leaning forward, I thought I could smell myself on him. I gave him a soft kiss on the lips, then I lay down, exhausted, pressed my body into his and draped an arm across his chest.

'Papa . . .' I whispered. 'Papa . . .'

Without warning, he gave a sharp mechanical start and stirred brusquely. He opened his eyes wide and jerked upright until he sat over me, gasping for breath. His body was violent and strange, a sudden colossus in shadow. He stared down for a long moment, breathing painfully, then formed his hands into a fist. I watched as he raised it shakily over his head. He opened his mouth wide and produced a long choking rattle. His old teeth emerged, and along with them that ancient sentry, his great tongue, sitting silently in his mouth. Our eyes locked in the dim light, and perhaps for the first time, he saw something of himself in me. His hands began to tremble and his arms flinched, high over his head.

I hesitated before reaching up and swaddling his doubled fist in my fingers. The struggle continued, brief, flagging, until I felt his muscles slacken and, finally, the old man surrendered. A tear formed on his cheek. He lowered his hands until they rested on my belly where I held them, warm, the knuckles pressing into my flesh. He sat like this, immobile, staring at me, his body shuddering. Tears were running down his cheeks and his chest heaved from the exertion. His silent sobs shook his figure and, brilliant against the light shining in from the bathroom, the ridgeline of white hairs along his arm and shoulder stood erect and fierce.

Solzhenitsyn in Vermont

I

ANTON SUGGESTED IT. HE SAID, HEAD TILTED BACK AND ARMS RAISED in a V of supplication to the changing weather, 'You don't get it. The game has rules. You're not supposed to be yourself. These girls want intensity, they want someone to talk big ideas. Books! Read all those weird writers with weirder names. That's the only way you'll get into these chicks' pants.'

In my time at Columbia I'd had no more than a handful of dates, with two ending drunkenly in unpleasant and fumbled lovemaking, where I felt like a deep-sea diver who had descended too far, too quickly, racing urgently to the surface.

'Start with Kafka,' Anton recommended, exhibiting a personal trainer's authority. 'He's hardcore.'

I was never much of a reader. In freshman comp I paid friends to write my papers or ordered them from an ad in the back pages of *The Village Voice*. Like most in my family, I was uninterested in the turmoil and dislocations I guessed literature examined. My father was a GP, born in Ludhiana, India, who came to New Jersey in the sixties and founded a small but thriving practice. Mom was a dentist from neighbouring Jullundar. The marriage was arranged, in the modern sense: they were allowed to meet several times and each decided they could live and, with luck, fall in love with the other. But instead of love, and after years of skirmishes and battles, an uneasy truce endured. My brother and I grew up in a simulacrum of stability, and I vowed at a young age that I'd do better, that this would never happen to me.

That night I read *The Metamorphosis*. Gregor Samsa's story immediately gripped me. How strange, funny, moving, yet also, I quickly recognized, how *possible*. Kafka had written something so outlandish it circled back, a ship sailing for a far continent that rounds the globe and returns home, and the story opened a door inside me to a room I never suspected was there.

Soon I was devouring one after another of his works, the novels, stories, parables, letters. At one store, I almost leapt on an elderly woman who reached for the sole copy of *Letters to Elena*. She must have sensed a feral quality in my eyes because she surrendered it without a word and hurried away. There were others: Dostoyevsky, Broch, Zweig or, in Anton's words, those weird writers with weirder names. The phone sat unanswered, dinner no more than the odd slice of pizza, and though I accomplished my coursework, all concentration rested on the books. Days passed without a shave, maybe not even a shower, and my clothes became a uniform, ratty jeans and a grey pullover.

No doubt I looked a fright because when Anton accosted me one afternoon on Broadway, he studied me with the surprise I'd expect him to reserve for something completely alien. We hadn't spoken since the day he recommended Kafka. In the meantime, I'd developed fraught and hushed relationships with bookdealers all across the island. These weren't friendships. There was always something predatory in our interactions, as though we were hunters circling each other. Yet these debilitated, suspicious old men and ironic slackers were the only people I could talk to as equals. They understood me in ways I could not express, with their secret boxes in far-off warehouses and promises of glowing rarities. I approached them as I would have approached priests, with fear, distaste and awe.

'What happened to you?' Anton cried out. 'How many times do I have to call?'

It was only then that he took notice of the books piled under my arm and rudely grabbed one, almost letting the others tumble to the sidewalk. 'What the fuck's all this, man—?' Then he did something which, for the first time in our friendship, deeply wounded me. He studied the cover, turned a few pages absently, and abruptly hoisted the book high into the air and began to laugh.

Because of that laugh, I never spoke to him again.

II

After graduation, I moved into a studio east of Avenue A and found a job consulting for an international accounting firm.

I devised statistical models projecting future efficiencies, given various scenarios. I shaved every day and dressed in a suit, yet constantly, at the back of my mind, I could sense that other me Anton had glimpsed, a dark creature haunting dusty, ill-lit rooms stacked high with unmarked boxes and searching for lost treasure. The furniture was sparse: futon on the floor, small desk, leather armchair, and a reading lamp found abandoned on the sidewalk the morning I moved in.

There were no bookshelves. I planned to watch books rise in towers around me, and finishing a book, say Goncharov's *Oblomov*, I'd snap it shut and place it on the nearest pile. A daydream: one day climbing onto a chair to reach my hand up to the ceiling to slide the final volume into a surrounding wall of books.

Luck with women continued to elude me. Even that final year at college, when girls jumped into friends' beds with the ease with which they hailed cabs on Amsterdam, I would put them off with my breathless excitement at discovering a new author. Sitting with my knees inching closer at a bar, I would suddenly ask, full of expectation, 'Bohumil Hrabal . . .?' or 'Bruno Schultz . . .?' as though the name phrased as a question explained itself. The evening universally slid downhill, tripping over the feet of my fervour and landing, unremarked, amid the crushed cigarettes staining the dark wood underfoot.

The morning Christie walked in to a meeting with a new client as one of my team members, I remember she was dressed in a peach business suit. She took the chair next to mine, introduced herself and, yawning, dropped her purse onto the desk next to a Styrofoam coffee cup. A crisp paperback nudged through the purse's open zipper. It was Kafka's *Metamorphosis*.

That night, over drinks, she asked, 'Do *you* write?'

She was the first person I confessed my dream to: a large, brightly lit study lined with bookshelves and overlooking a garden of acacia and spruce, maybe a stream, and long, unadorned pine tables, the kind Solzhenitsyn wrote on in his hideaway in Vermont, where I would complete a single great work, a novel to stand beside the masterpieces I adored.

Soon we were seeing each other almost every night.

One evening, sitting together on the love seat in her West Side apartment, we discussed Dostoyevsky's *Crime and Punishment*. She'd been turned off by the book at first. She couldn't understand why Raskolnikov murdered the old pawn broker, and she understood less the frightful hell his actions caused him to descend into.

'He's some idiot-savant,' she said. 'He has no clue what he's doing and he just keeps digging a bigger and bigger hole for himself!'

She'd warmed to the book only after Sonia Semyonovna's appearance, confessing with a drunken sway and a furrowing of her brows, that it confirmed a deeply held belief of hers. She meant the *necessity of suffering*. Not suffering on the scale of Raskolnikov's—a person shouldn't have to murder an old woman to find some answer to questions in their life! But it offered a grand vision, a life so much larger than itself, as if it were projected onto an oversized, multiplex screen, though in her mind she didn't see a static screen, but a sheet of white canvas rustling in the breeze. This way, parts of the image fell in and out of focus. The lesson she drew from the book was that suffering was a constant companion, however small or large your life was. Maybe *necessity* was the wrong word and, now she thought about it, she preferred *companion*. Yes, she said, that's closer, the *companionship of suffering*. Look at Raskolnikov, he was an ass, a murderer, totally self-involved. Look what he had to go through just to have a glimmer of true feeling for Sonia! But she stood by him and the reason was not some outdated notion of a woman standing by her man, but because she saw that through him, they could together arrive at something essential! She thought it unspeakably romantic, and often while she was reading, she'd think of herself as Sonia. Would it be so terrible, she asked, to have been alive then under those circumstances?

I'd thought just that: myself as Raskolnikov. Not the murderer, except in a sort of way, the man who murdered the old woman, the Raskolnikov bewildered by the world, thinking it low, hypocritical, who believed himself set apart! There was something of that in me, I confessed. 'I get the feeling somewhere, something went wrong. A sort of crazy mistake. This isn't me, this world isn't mine. I don't know which.'

She raised her glass and offered in a funny, grave voice, 'Then I will be your Sonia,' clinking glasses, 'and you my Raskolnikov!'

That's when I did a surprising thing, a surprise even to myself. I placed a hand firmly on her thigh and looked into her eyes, and said, 'Will you be *my* Sonia? Will you marry me?'

III

Within months, we'd put a down payment on a four-bedroom on Long Island. Every morning, I promised, I'd commute in, reading on the LIRR and return home every night to write. Work on the dream study progressed rapidly. Knocking out a wall between two bedrooms opened a grand space where we installed bay windows overlooking not acacia and spruce but an aged and dying oak. Ceiling-high shelves lined the walls with sliding ladders along each section and I commissioned the pine table from a Japanese woodworker on West 17th. The table took close to a year to complete and arrived in time for our first anniversary.

The marriage, as rapidly, faltered.

We clashed over bills, cooking, chores, the diminished time we spent together, our deflated suburban lives. The commute offered me no peace. People barked into cell phones, others snored, the smell of breakfast burritos pervaded the cars, the train conductors clicked tickets incessantly. My work responsibilities expanded and soon I returned home later every night, tapping out not great stories on the train but memos on office etiquette.

Far into the evening, I would sit alone in the study, nursing a whisky and reflecting on my purposeless days and the increasing strains with Christie. The broad, custom-built table scolded me. I had not written a word, not imagined what I might ever write. Recessed lights in the ceiling lit the room brightly but obscured the garden, painting the windows black and hiding the broad gloom beyond. Out in the suburban darkness, I sometimes sensed shapes moving, animals, prowlers, strange beings. Figures formed in the blackness and I gave to them my darkest imagination: something was out there, hunting me, drawing ever closer, a creature on the scent of my disorder, a monster of chaos, with only one thought in its head: my annihilation.

The plan first offered itself to me as a means to fend off this terror. It was a preposterous idea, and I brushed it away without thought. But there it was, nightly reappearing, and during those shapeless nights when I sensed the dim thud of a phantom step, I would sit and stare at my surrounding morgue of books with rising discomfort and fear. I'd come to believe, in my lonely bachelor nights, that a book without a reader is a dead book. I'd even feel a dread pass through my body on finishing one and consigning it to the piles leaning against walls. That dread now echoed throughout this room. Was that it? Was that the scent of death the creature stiffened at? My marriage was a failure, this room that I'd had such hopes for was no more than a child's playroom in a childless couple's home, and my own days were unfulfilled and compassless. Something had to be done.

This was the idea. I would hire a reader, someone to read these books during the day while I was at work. He'd be another me. He'd sit in this room and read, read everything. And in the evenings we would talk, and sometimes Christie would join us, and we'd be an eccentric and happy threesome.

If I could save the books, I reasoned, I would salvage the rest of it, the marriage, my sense of self. I'd even be given, as if miraculously, the time and will to write my book.

IV

John invariably wore a white T-shirt and jeans and I clocked his daily late-morning arrival by having him call my cell from the home phone. Caller ID placed him there. How he spent the rest of the day, at least until Christie returned home, I accepted on trust. Sometimes I would call and speak calmly into the answering machine. 'John, are you there . . .?' Only twice did I have to wait over a minute before he picked up, and when he reached the phone he was panting. 'What's going on?' I asked. 'Nothing. Just reading,' he replied without concern.

My hope was he'd stay some nights until I returned, because not only did I want to know what he read, but I wanted to hear his thoughts, to listen to him compare and discuss my many books. I was surprised when our meetings turned out to be simple, almost clinical affairs, closer to interrogations than brotherly chats. John gave brief and to-the-point answers and our relationship, to my confusion, never developed beyond those I had with my own assistants. Even after months, I lacked the courage to ask John to call me by my first name. This wasn't how I'd imagined it. I had hoped we would sit together like college buddies over a bottle of scotch, talking late into the night of things that matter.

Christie viewed the exercise as grossly irresponsible. It

was ludicrous, bordering on the pathological, to think a book without a reader is a dead book, and worse, to imagine a reader might somehow salvage our faltering marriage. She wanted us to enter therapy, she suggested we go on dates together, as though we were again an unmarried couple, or that I read to her, the way I had when we first met. All practical suggestions, I agreed, but none could solve the essential problem, whose full outline even I didn't understand. The great stories did not resolve their conflicts through everyday solutions, so why should not a life, my life, have found structure in the tangents of narrative, in the unseen influence of shadowed myths?

Then one day at the office, I slipped my wedding ring off and placed it in my desk drawer and asked Jenna, a new intern and a senior at Columbia, to join me for a drink after work. I was shocked at myself, at my own sudden ability for action, and as I walked along the corridor to her cubicle, as I spoke, as I waited for her response, it was as if another man was standing in my body. Her short black hair, the stud in her nose, her loose, sensual clothes reminded me of the women I once chased but never caught, women with the irresistible aura of unknown, bohemian lives.

We cabbed it to an old Second Avenue haunt of mine where I had always come alone and left alone. In the intervening years, it had transformed. Gone were the impoverished characters I remembered. Now the place was high-end, video screens on the walls, drinks more than double the price.

Three rounds and we were both laughing, and the sudden

ease left me feeling elated. Who were these women who had terrorized my student lusts? Did they care about the books I loved? Did they read the ones they carried so elegantly to and from coffeeshops? Finally, I had to do it. Placing a hand on her thigh and letting my fingers run perilously close to her crotch, I said it, the question that had doomed one date after another, what Anton called the weird name of a weirder writer: '*Bohumil Hrabal*?'

She stopped, drink in midair, and stared at me. A moment later she exploded into peals of laughter, thrusting the glass high over her head and rocking back and forth on the stool, until eventually, returning the drink to the counter, she wrapped a hand around my neck and pulled me close.

'I'm fucking sorry,' she said, her lips brushing my earlobe. 'I didn't mean that. I didn't mean to laugh. I couldn't help myself. But is that how they talk where you come from?'

It was my turn to laugh. 'Yes,' I nodded vigorously. 'Yes yes!' Exultant, I repeated a stream of nonsense syllables and soon Jenna was almost toppling off her stool, she was laughing so hard.

That's when I reached out a hand, enclosed her waist, pulled her to me and kissed her.

I phoned Christie from my mobile, holding it close to my mouth as I stood in the restroom to drown the noise from the bar, and told her I'd be sleeping at the office. Soon I was sleeping at the office once a week, sometimes more. There wasn't only Jenna. The old campus bars where I'd suffered one rejection after another proved now to be excellent hunting ground for co-eds and soon I discovered how easy it was to pick up a young student, take her to a hotel room, and never talk to or see her again. The remaining evenings with Christie left me strangely lighter, as though in our time together I was floating a few inches above her, bobbing on the puffs of our spare conversation. During our dinners together we talked shop, she new accounting models, me statistical challenges. When this flagged, it'd be office politics, frustrations during the day, whether to rent a movie or watch the box. Sex happened when we found ourselves in bed together with nothing else to do. It became, to my surprise, an enjoyable life.

Jenna's laugh had murdered the haunted reader in me. Unlike Anton's derisive laughter, Jenna's hid nothing. Sharp, clear, deadly, it punctured the old me to the heart, and in seconds, that man was gone. I looked back with a shudder on who I had been. I'd never understood the books I read. I'd read greedily, checking the clock to count the pages, growing disgusted if I found it too little. When I closed one, I'd reach immediately for another, leaving no time to contemplate or digest. It was a constant battle to read more and I lived in a continual fever of words.

Then one evening, when I arrived home late as usual, Christie met me in the kitchen. She asked if I'd eaten, and I said yes, at one of those Indo/Pak taxi delis on the West Side, and I poured myself a scotch and only then did I see she was staring at me with a hard, intent glare. An argument, I thought, and wondered what I'd done. But she didn't want to argue. She had only one thing to say. She wanted a divorce.

That night I slept in the study, bundled in heavy sheets,

sensing, even in my dreams, the breath of that phantom hunter, the creature in the night, as step by step it drew ever closer.

V

I woke sweating, still in my clothes and wrapped so tightly I could hardly breathe. The sun sliced in through the windows, filtered by the leaves of the oak, and the room looked brilliant and alive and perturbed.

The night before, I'd telephoned John and told him not to come in today, that I would drop by and visit him. I didn't say why, I wasn't sure myself. Christie's demand hit me hard, and I thought if I lost her, I would lose everything, myself included. Action was needed, a violent break with my past, to show Christie I might yet be the man she married.

John greeted me in a white T-shirt and boxers and on opening the door, retreated into the darkness of the kitchen. A bed stood near the window at one end of the long, narrow apartment, while a desk held a computer with the remaining free space buried under books and papers. A large, brightly coloured painting hung on the wall, unframed, the canvas edges irregular and worn, and a beaten-up sofa sat opposite with a crate substituting for a table holding on it an overflowing ashtray and three coffee mugs.

'Pretty different,' he said, returning with coffee. 'From yours, I mean.'

'I used to live nearby in a place even smaller.'

Gone now was the forced stiffness, the sense that I was the

employer and he the employee, and the change unsettled me, leaving me uncertain where to start. I'd thought it out on the train, what I was going to say, how exactly I would phrase it, but now all my plans were slipping rapidly away.

'Are you an artist?' I asked stupidly. 'Or a writer?'

'No. I do freelance web design. The market's cold these days for the independent guy. Your gig was a fucking godsend.'

'The economy?'

'Uh huh.' He produced a tin box and opened it. 'Joint?' he asked.

I shook my head and he lit one for himself. The smoke filtered through the room and I changed my mind and reached out and took a long drag, then another. Instead of relaxing me, the drug caused my body to stiffen and a sharp ache spread through my back.

'Careful, it's strong.'

'Uh huh.'

Turning to the computer, he said, 'Do you want to see?'

'What?'

'My sites. The money's in porn these days.'

A sudden fury rose in me and I decided I hated John, that I always had, and I wanted nothing more at that moment than to strike him. I decided to come directly to the point.

'I know,' I said. 'I know everything.'

He looked confused. 'About what?'

'You and Christie. She told me last night. The affair, how long it's been going on, the smallest details. She said she couldn't stand the lies anymore. She was in tears.'

I was hoping for a fight. He'd protest, I'd accuse, sooner or later he'd be driven to rage and come flying at me. And I'd be the one defending Christie. It was ritual combat I was after, a duel for Christie's honour. What were all those books about, I'd thought last night lying alone in the study, but duels moved to the page? The author against his past, the words against the author, the characters against each other, the reader against everyone. These were battles to the death, shifted from their ancient arenas, the colloseums, the jousting fields, the forest glades, and moved onto an inner theatre. Everything happened within, and it was a cheat, I thought, a stupid, lowdown swindle! Where was the blood? No one saw it. No one actually died. My mistake was that I'd believed them, these books, that if you read them they would change a life! It was all crass bunk. What I wanted was the real thing, real blood, John's blood.

He sat back in his chair studying me, first with bafflement, then with a grin widening on his lips.

'Do you have anything to say for yourself?' I said.

'I don't know what you're talking about.'

'Oh, come on! She's told me everything! Don't lie. I'm not here to fight with you. I want to know what's going on.'

'She said we were . . . what? Fucking?'

'If you want to put it so bluntly, yes.'

'I don't know what she told you, but it's not true.' Then with a laugh, he added, 'I don't know what this is about. She's a beautiful woman, I'll admit I was tempted. But no way it's true.' He paused and looked across the room, toward the window, lost in thought, and finally said, 'Who knows? Maybe she suspects something about you.'

'Don't be an idiot. This is about you and my wife.'

'Is it?'

There was nothing else for it. I decided to launch into the speech I'd practised on the train.

'When I hired you, it wasn't as some employee or office flunky. You had the run of my house and my absolute trust, and all you had to do was read my books. Those aren't ordinary books, those aren't sweet airs and lullabies, throwaway paperbacks from the mall bookstore. When you read one of those books, the book makes you a promise. It holds a tradition between its pages, one that goes back for generations. If you accept the promise, the book lets you become part of that tradition. Even as an ordinary reader, you're joining on equal footing. This is what I gave you. You didn't hold up your part of the deal, did you? No, what you did was—'

I stopped, because there was John, laughing at me. The laugh began as a smirk, but grew quickly, and soon he was almost toppling from his chair, roaring.

'What is it?' I demanded. 'What the fuck are you laughing at?' The moment I asked him, his face changed and I felt a deep alarm ringing inside me.

'Do I have to spell it out? One of my oldest friends is Susan Caulfield, you know, little Susie. She's told me everything.'

A sickening chill ran through me. Susie was one of the girls I'd picked up at one of my new haunts. I'd told her I was a writer, that much of the time I needed to be closeted in my Long Island atelier. She hated the subterfuge and the rationed time we spent together. It ended when she threw a drink in my face at a downtown club and stormed out.

'I don't know what you mean,' I said, pushing my fears aside, and stood and approached the painting while John's eyes followed me. It was a nude, maybe it was Susie, I thought strangely. The woman, though highly abstracted, seemed to be falling. I could feel myself entering the brush strokes, as though the surface created by the layers of paint was a second work embedded in the first, offering a private geography, almost another world that, for a brief moment, allowed me to escape from this one. I rode down low on the broad lines of paint, sliding into the gullies and rising to plateaus and peaks, only to descend again into those shadowy realms.

'I don't know any Susan . . . what's her name?'

'Oh, for chrissakes, give it up! I'm no fucking snitch, man, if that's what this is about. What you do is your fucking business. I don't know what's going on with you. Why you came here, what this story with Christie's about, whatever.' He shook his head, and added, 'There's a lot you've got to learn if you're going to play the game. First, don't give them the rundown on your conquests. It doesn't help.'

Instantly, and without thinking, I threw myself at him. It was a sudden, instinctual fury, an act I hadn't contemplated a moment before. I lunged blindly, wanting to smash into his body with all the force of mine. That's not what happened. My foot caught the edge of the crate and both it and I went careening. We missed each other completely and I slammed my head violently into the corner of the desk and doubled back, screaming and in agony, and collapsed into a ball squirming on the floor.

'You fucking maniac!' John cried. He jumped from his chair and I could hear him stalking angrily from one end of the apartment to the other, repeating that phrase over and over.

The pain subsided quickly. When I pulled my fingers away, their tips were bloodied. I lay there, listening to John's feet strike the hardwood floor and his angry breath roiling across the room. He picked up the phone, dropped it again into its cradle, then I listened as he gathered the shattered fragments of mugs and ashtray and I was washed over with an odd sympathy for this man that only moments before I hated and I wished more than anything that I could tell him that and not simply lie there, my eyes tight shut, shivering and afraid.

VI

The lunch-time streets belched up their crowds as I navigated my way toward the subway. Before I left, John wordlessly handed me a towel and a box of Band-Aids and these, standing crouched under the sloping ceiling of his bathroom, I applied with shaking hands to the gash on my forehead, without once facing myself in the mirror. On reaching the street, all memory of walking the three flights down vanished, though I'd accomplished it seconds before. Well, I thought, tugging what little satisfaction I could from that loose-willed exhibition, I have blood, and with that, I can say something to Christie. But what? The struggle itself, I thought, I'll describe the struggle. I will tell it as something new, imaginary. I will tell her a story that will announce the depth of my love.

That was when a strange thing happened. Someone struck me hard on the arm and hurried quickly on. It was a young woman who turned for a moment and held me with a look of contempt. Her dark hair fell nearly to the middle of her back and she could easily have been Indian or Puerto Rican or Greek. Meeting her eyes caused an electrifying sensation to spirit through my body and she turned immediately away and without thinking I followed after her, hurrying to catch up. We passed a gaudy row of Indian restaurants with their strings of lights and made a right onto Second Avenue. Her shabby jeans, her red revealing top, thrilled through every step I took and I followed close behind, barely a step or two, so near I could smell her hair. She turned again and only after she stopped did I realize where she had led me: my old street. We stood together at the foot of my one-time home, that tiny studio where I once dreamt of stacking books like an enclosing wall. I was inches away as she slipped the key into the lock and twisted it, pushed the door in and on entering, held it wide for me, like a tamer holding open a lion's massive jaws, and immediately I knew I was home.

Five flights up and me a step behind her every moment, tasting the sharp odour of her sweat as it pressed through the air toward me. The stairwell graffiti had changed little over the years and we wound up through the stiff artery of creaking steps as if toward a fractured heart. The old door to my apartment hung in the gloom at the end of the hall where all lights had long since been broken, and once there, standing at this familiar portal, I pressed my body against her back and waited, my own heart thumping and my lips touching the nape of her neck, until the door swung open and we were, in moments, swallowed by even deeper darkness. A black blanket covered the single window, the floors were crowded with refuse, and the bed was simply a mattress with a metal headboard and footboard and no sheets. Broken, leaning against a wall, stood the lamp I had found on the corner the morning I first moved in. Once inside, she moved quickly, gathering up objects and only after several minutes did she approach me and motioned with her eyes to my clothes. I stripped off in a state of excitement and then she looked at the bed and I lay down on it. We didn't say a word.

Reaching across my body, she pulled one of my wrists fiercely up and tied it with a leather strip to the bedpost. The moment she touched me, I knew, with a certainty beyond words, that we were the same person, and it wasn't me she was tying, but that I was doing this to myself. Her breast pressed against my face as she tied the leather off and pulled it taut until the band cut almost into the bone. In minutes, I was spread-eagled on the bed, wrists and ankles already humming in soft pain. She climbed onto me and forced an old rag into my mouth and tied it into place with something like a belt. The rag smelled vile and it was all I could do not to choke on it, but moments later, my situation became more dire. I was blindfolded and masked and could hardly breathe except through tiny holes for my nose. Struggling, I threw my head back and to the side, and immediately felt her mouth press against the side of my shrouded head and for the first time I heard her voice: a gentle, consoling whisper of a breath, and instantly, all fight left me. Soon, she was moving again, pulling the bonds tighter at my feet and arms. I lay there, unresponsive, allowing the pain to slice deeper into my flesh, for were we not the same person, the same body, one and the same agony? She will leave me alone to die, I thought, for that was what I would have done to myself, here, caught in a mad web, naked and in pain, adrift on ever rising waves as if my body floated farther and farther out, and I was already a corpse waiting for the rot of my flesh to be discovered. Instead I felt her move close to me with some object, a knife perhaps, and she jabbed it, creating a hole at my ear, making sure to nip the side of my head, and then there was her miraculous breath pulsing against me in soft, startled whispers.

She was singing an old lullaby, 'Rock-a-bye-baby'. Her voice rang out with an otherworldly confidence, as if she had landed here, on this planet, in this age, to do exactly this, to sing this song to me in my time of distress and terror. Above me, the sky opened and my body, which now floated on the epidermis of the oceans, was nothing more than so much flotsam and jetsam in a whole universe of castaways. There were other songs, so many, some I knew, others new to me. 'Tom Dooley' and 'Mr Bojangles' and 'I Shall be Released' and the hours passed and became days, and the days passed and became years, and on that bed, all flesh fell away, the blood dried up, and I was transformed into something harder and substantive, an alloy, a severe and glinting metal.

When I woke she was gone and the restraints released and I lay there naked on that bed in a state of enchantment. It was some time before I could stand, shaking, nauseous, hungry, and I ran into a corner and vomited violently. Straightening again and searching for my clothes in a slow circle around the room, I experienced a sense of defeat, but over what, by whom, what battles had I ever fought? Eventually I discovered my watch resting on the dresser. According to it, no more than an hour had passed. I was sure it was wrong. I was certain beyond doubt it had been years.

VII

'Do you want a drink?' Christie said. She didn't look at me when I walked into the kitchen. Instead, her back to me, she was pouring herself a glass of white wine. I had been sitting in the study, watching the garden darken and the colours shift, the green taking on the burden of night while the eastern sky inked over, greedily inhaling a whole palette of colours before losing itself to black. When I heard her, the key in the lock, the pad of steps along the hall, I felt a momentary desire to tell her everything, the whole sorry story from my confusion when I asked her to marry me to all the events of today. The impulse was sudden, and I squashed it as suddenly, but walking down the stairs to meet her in the kitchen, the thought continued to float at the far edge of my consciousness.

'I'll get it,' I said, stepping in behind her and reaching around for the scotch. I thrust the glass at the ice dispenser and watched five cubes splash into the drink while Christie turned and looked at me. I raised the glass to my lips.

'What happened to your face? You look awful.'

'It doesn't matter. Some kid on a skateboard decided not to look where he was going.'

'Let me see.'

'No, don't.'

'Fine,' she said, irritated. 'Have it your way.' She turned and began her nightly search of the refrigerator to see if there was anything to eat.

'There's never a goddam thing, is there?'

'The fall was nothing, okay,' I said. 'A guy in a shop patched me up. It's not important. What's important is that I want to talk to you tonight. I want to try and explain.'

She folded her arms, dropped her chin until she was staring at her feet and stood like that, silently tapping one foot. She said, 'Okay, we talk.'

We were soon settled side by side on the living-room sofa, each with a drink, staring at the sliding glass doors leading to a hardwood deck we almost never used, and a garden which was pretty much alien territory for the both of us. The television was Christie's old one, as was the glass coffee table where I had earlier placed a copy of Dostoyevsky's *Crime and Punishment*. Her copy, a hardbound Modern Library edition with a worn blue cover whose pages were warped by water. She'd told me, on one of our early dates, that she had dropped it in the bathtub one night when reading, and I'd felt a tremendous warmth for her, for someone who'd lie in a tub and actually read that book.

'I don't know what's happened to me these past few months,' I said.

'Months?'

'What? You want an exact date? An anniversary?'

'No. Go on.'

'When I look in the mirror, I don't recognize myself. I'm not the man you married, I don't know why.'

'*And* . . . so what's the news here? You think I'm surprised? I don't know who you are either. I have no fucking clue!'

'Please, Christie, let me try and explain.'

'No . . . you wait. If this is going where I think it's going, I don't want stories. I don't want to hear how much you love me, how fucking sorry you are, how it'll all be different. It's too late.'

Perhaps that's what I would have tried had I come straight to meet her from my encounter with John, but the events of the afternoon had changed everything. I was already beginning to question whether it really happened—the coincidence seemed too striking: my old apartment, a sadistic siren . . . But what then is reality, I asked myself, if not the coagulation of past circumstance and a person's present. It is the inexplicable that claims the heart, that shapes us every day, for better or worse. Don't we lay these traps for ourselves every minute? Simply by living, by acting in the world, we erect a history that must, sooner or later, overpower and strangle us. These were the thoughts I had as I sat alone waiting for Christie, and this was why, if there can be any reason, I chose my curious love song.

'I had an idea,' I said. 'I thought I'd try to read to you like I used to. I wanted to try and make things better, back to the way they used to be.'

She looked down at the copy of *Crime and Punishment*.

'*That?*'

'What's wrong with it? It's one of your favourites.'

'It is, but . . .'

'Please,' I said.

Christie brought her bare feet onto the sofa and leaned her back against the armrest. She was looking directly at me. She pulled her legs to her chest and balanced the half-empty glass on one knee.

The chapter I'd picked was from Part Two, set after the murder, when Raskolnikov is delirious from a fever and is certain everyone suspects him. He wanders through the city, passing drunks and whores and, stopping at the Palais de Cristal, meets Zametov, the head clerk at the police station. It was this same Zametov who earlier watched Raskolnikov faint when the murder was discussed, and Raskolnikov knew the head clerk believed him to be the killer.

I had never really understood what Christie meant when she spoke about suffering that night we became engaged, but it was her words then that prompted me now, which pushed me forward to read aloud the section I chose. The mental leap she made then, the one from *necessity* to *companionship*, was what I wanted her to think about. If she could see that, if she could see us continuing together, like Sonia with Raskolnikov, then I suspected I still had one last chance to avert the disaster of my parents' marriage.

But once I started reading, I forgot about everything, where I was, what I was really trying to do, and I identified completely with the voice of Raskolnikov. I found myself fully inside his being. I could see myself walking along the same streets he walked, and when he entered a loud throng, I heard the noises, the people, the singing. My legs shuddered when he stepped over a drunk. And once Zametov appeared, my whole face transformed. It was as though I was possessed. I took on every grimace, every sharp look, every whispered word as though I was the killer himself.

I was exhausted when I finished, shut the book, replaced it on the table and fell back against the cushions and closed my eyes. Every feature of my face must have spoken directly of that Raskolnikov she so admired, every nuance of deception and knowledge, every falsehood stacked upon falsehood. Even at the end, when Raskolnikov's face was trembling, hysterical and twisted, mine was equally so, a vision of a man pulled out of hell, and it was this man, the *one who suffers*, that I was sure Christie would see and sympathize with. She'd understand, she'd know, we too could be that unhappy, suffering couple, Raskolnikov and Sonia, just as we had once promised each other in that single brief moment of our love.

Days seemed to pass before I had the courage to open my eyes again. I was startled by a sound from the garden, a branch cracking in the night. When finally I looked across, Sonia was gone. Only one glass remained. Mine. Even the side of the sofa where she had curled herself into a ball appeared as if it had never been touched. She was like a cat sometimes. A ghostly silence had fallen over the house. The sound of wood cracking in the distance returned and I walked to the glass doors and stood, staring out at the garden, the patch of light on the hardwood deck, shivering for reasons I didn't understand.

The sound of cracking branches drew closer. It was as if the trees were being shaken and crushed by something approaching. I interrogated the darkness and after a minute I could make out a great black shape. The trees trembled against the starlight, and soon, the stars began to disappear, one by one, as the great shape menaced toward me. The lights of houses blinked out and the glow of the distant city, always there, now appeared at the edges of my vision as the creature seemed to grow wider and taller with every shuddering step.

Finally, emerging from the dense, shattered woodland at the far end of the garden, there appeared a colossus of a man, so huge he hid the sky behind him. He was heading directly for me. The ground trembled as he approached. He had come to destroy me, he had come to rid the world of me, he was my annihilator. His breath shook the glass from a hundred feet away. The ringing boom of his heart slapped against the soles of my feet. I got down on my knees, waiting for the blow from his massive fist. Whole minutes passed with me expecting it at every moment, hearing his steps grow closer until the house was shaking free from its foundations and the sound of his feet thundered in my ears. I heard him mount the deck and the wood cracked underfoot and I thought, this is my last moment.

Nothing happened. After a minute I gathered my courage and looked up.

There he was, a great dim shadow visible faintly through the glass. His trunk-like legs were illuminated by light from the living room. The deck was wrecked, crushed below his massive weight, and he towered far above me and the house. I strained my neck and stared up until I could peer into his enormous face, and that was when I saw, for the first of many times, my dear, tragic companion, that blasted frown, those great eyes anguished and sad, and only moments later did it become clear to me that he was weeping.

Neanderthal Tongues

I CAN TRACE IT BACK THAT FAR. IT WAS ISMAIL'S DEATH THAT REVEALED the grammar of the landscape, that allowed me to understand the meaning of the flat desert plain as it fell into the disorder of the badlands.

In Ethiopia, inland from the slim ribbon of beach along the Red Sea, the land rises to a high levee of mountains that hoard what little rain comes down. A desert plain flattens the continent before it splits and falls into the Great Rift. It is here—a realm of gullies and valleys, of infinite variation, yet linked by a communal disarray—that the world is pulling apart.

I am dead, and below me water shuffles into darkness. Contrary to superstition in which the dead become universal—no up, no down, just a bland everything—there is a below me, as there is an above me, and a me. Land is nowhere to be seen—only the wreckage of the plane, fragments of burnt and twisted wing, seat cushions, their springs popping out, the aftermath of what could have been a victory parade: torn barf bags like confetti, magazines, newspapers, boarding passes, passports. And sometimes the dead on the parade route, or at least pieces of them, their limbs, their eyes. I am better at knowing the bones, the small fragments of zygomatic arch, the lumbar vertebrae shattered.

Ismail joined me in Ethiopia that summer. It was the first and only expedition I ever led, a coveted prize after two years teaching at Michigan, and before that, as a graduate student in physical anthropology when I worked on surveys in Pakistan and Kenya.

We were a small team. I was denied NSF funding. A new professor, and though my thesis was published, it was far from groundbreaking and I was thought unproven. Only those students who won travel grants on their own merits were able to accompany me. There were five of us, and a cook. Three were graduate students from Michigan: Bill, Ellen and Steve.

Ismail was the sole Ethiopian among us. He would start as one of my graduate students the following term, and we met him in Addis Ababa. We had planned a preliminary mapping of an area in the north, along the eastern rim of the Great Rift, a bare reconnaissance of the badlands whose thick fingers extended to the far horizon. A team of petroleum geologists who travelled through the area two years earlier had collected fossil mammal remains that suggested the region had exposed layers almost two million years old.

That first night in the desert found us all marvelling at the stars, our blanket, at the stillness of a universe that had retracted from us only to show its distant splendour. The cook's heavy breath as he turned the goat on its spit, the fire bursting open the night—I remember the smells, the sounds. We argued about Binford and Isaac, about the significance of recent excavations. When the fire sputtered, we thought the stars might blind us.

The following day Ismail saw a thin string of smoke in the distance, rising like an exclamation, but the cook had laughed at the city boy. Those were just hunters, he said. Ismail said nothing. Only later did he tell me of the rumours of the widening war, of trouble in the north. We would never have been given our permit had there been the possibility of trouble, I explained, there was nothing to worry about. Ismail's eyes continued to reflect the horizon, though he never spoke of it again.

My father, Hukum, had told me about his village in India. I had never been to India. I was born one cold winter in New York, and in those first few weeks, my mother told me, the pipes had rattled in the apartment building until finally they burst. Water flooded the first floor and became ice, and the firemen used blowtorches to melt their way into our building. My father said that in India they gave names to the dark spaces between the stars. It was the darkness that was novel, scarce, that seemed brilliant against so much light. Sometimes I would find my father late at night in the living room, the lights all off, only the clock glowing on the VCR. He would say that it was such a relief, this darkness, this not being able to see. Only years later did I learn what it was he was hoping not to see.

My body spreads every day, the currents and the horizon of cold waves pushing me in different directions. One hour, one part of me is warmed by the red breaking of dawn, while another still misses the recent evening. Soon night and day will be eternal, dawn and sunset constants from which I will never be free. Sharks tear at pieces of me, at the water snake of my intestine, the sweet of my testicle, and in the distance there are screams—faraway terrors, growing closer. One eyeball sinks to the ocean floor and is caught up in warm currents rising from an underwater volcano.

Immediately after the explosion, when my body was blown into—how many, I don't know, maybe a hundred thousand, maybe a million—fragments, I had the illusion that I was everywhere at once. That every part of me—every smallest fragment, from the length of my femur to the stray spots of blood suddenly red, diluting—was connected. Not in the physical sense, the way a body is naturally connected, but through our senses. It is hard to find a correct pronoun for the experience—we, us, I, it? In those seconds I saw everything that every part of me saw, experienced everything from all the diverse views that a splintered body possesses. I was at one with all the elements of my body for the first time. For a few seconds, I understood them and understood their sudden and enlarging fear—my own fear—as within moments our consciousness began to deflate.

It lasted only seconds, as though we were living in the aftermath of a camera flash, slowly fading, the light dimming, and I soon lost touch with the lines of my veins, the fragments of appendix, the small bones of the hand, the drowning balls of spit and urine.

The expedition was almost over. We had found no evidence of hominid remains, but many of the fossils we did recover suggested that in future seasons, with a larger team and more intensive surveys, this area could prove fruitful. Ismail and I were walking. The high sun hid our shadows under our feet. When we came to the last gully, his face was weary and sweat glinted off his skin like jewels. I'll take this side, I said, you that. He nodded. He had been distracted all morning, said he had heard a gunshot in the night. But on the two-way radio back into town, there was no news of any trouble. There were the regular skirmishes farther north of us, but nothing where we were.

We'll be finished in three days, I said, and then you fly with us to the States. He smiled at this, and I let the weight of my body pull me down into a gully, showering the air with fine white dust. Up on the ridgeline, he was watching me. I saw his silhouette, hesitant. In a week, I shouted up, Michigan!

Super Bowl and McDonald's! Ismail shouted back. His body slid down into the next gully over.

An hour later, I was halfway along the cleavage of this ancient wound, finding nothing visible, when I heard his scream and the shouts of strange voices. Then Ismail again, his throat scrabbling for air.

When my parents moved to New York, my father already spoke English well, though haltingly. My mother's English was poor, and she was excited at the possibility of improving it. She wanted both of them to take ESL classes at City College, but my father refused to listen to the idea. He said that they (meaning *him,* according to my mother) spoke English more than well enough to get by. He said they would both take classes in Esperanto, which—my father claimed—was the language of the future; in a decade, everyone would be speaking it. It was language, he told my mother, that had ripped India apart, thrown it into the pool of communal violence. How can a country persist—a world even—where people cannot speak to each other? This was his argument.

This was when my mother was pregnant with me and in her fury she almost took his head off with her fist. It was the pregnancy, the sudden mood swings, the new country. She slammed her fist into his face, knocking him down onto the carpet, bloodying his nose.

See! he shouted from where he lay on the floor, Until we all speak one language, we will always fight.

All argument fled my mother with that single blow. She was not a violent person and was shocked at herself. It was not the weight of my father's belief but of her own violence that persuaded her to go along with him and learn Esperanto before she mastered English. When I was still small, I remember her voice, sometimes late at night, singing me songs and nursery rhymes in a language I barely remember, a language I have never since heard anyone else speak.

Still, she remained firm on one point. She made sure I was never forced to speak that language. They taught me English and Hindi instead, and I was allowed only those few words of Esperanto picked up by chance from the two of them. It was a strange household, all of us speaking different languages. My father clung to Esperanto, my mother to Hindi, and I managed a patois of these two and English. It was the farthest from my father's dream of a common language I can imagine.

One night, I remember, they were arguing—both shouting in Esperanto. My five-year-old self could see them clearly, the small shelf of books behind my father, the black-and-white TV flickering, the smell of milk on the stove in the kitchen. *What* they were saying to each other was beyond me, but it was the last night my mother ever spoke Esperanto in the house. At one point, my father was on the verge of striking her. I could see his hand formed into a fist. At that moment, my mother let out a scream—the only time I ever heard her scream, a scream in no language I knew. It wasn't a Hindi scream or an English scream—I have heard those—and I am certain it wasn't an Esperanto scream, because no one would resort to so foreign a language at such a moment. It was something else entirely, and it stopped my father's fist midair. Stunned, he stood motionless for a moment—then his body slumped, relaxed, and he put his arms around her, talking softly in Hindi.

Three men surrounded Ismail, all shouting, all with rifles. In my panic I had scrambled up and over the thigh of rock that separated our two small valleys, dirt catching under my nails, my breath suddenly hard. The gunmen wore jeans, old, beaten athletic shoes, dirty T-shirts. Thick ammo belts hung across their chests, as though they were old-time bandits. One brought down the butt of his rifle like a bat, smashing it against Ismail's head and the young man fell to the ground, screaming, a pool of blood already forming on the dry desert surface.

Who the fuck are you? I shouted down, and three faces turned to acknowledge me, mouths rigid and tense. The action of a rifle click echoed across the landscape and suddenly, looking down there, at guns now pointed up at me, I wanted nothing more than to scramble back down into the hot gully I had emerged from, to abandon Ismail to his murderers without a thought. I didn't see the one who aimed at me, instead I heard the gunshot and my body flew back, tumbling into the white of the gully, dust in my mouth, the taste of blood. I screamed.

My body curled into a ball, trembling, and my mother's scream that night many years before filled my ears. I remember it now as above me clouds have cut the stars away from me, and a storm rumbles in this direction, already tossing parts of me around, viciously. My mother's long-ago scream had seemed incomprehensible, as though something ancient were shouting through her. But when I heard Ismail's—and heard my own echoing through my skull—something in me understood the origin of that scream. I lay at the bottom of the gully, shaking, terrified, certain already that Ismail would be killed. Why—? I didn't know and didn't care. My mouth was full of blood and above me the blueness of the sky, my only companion, appeared like a glove strangling me.

At the camp, Steve, one of my graduate students who had been briefly in medical school, dressed the wound. The bullet hadn't penetrated the skin, had simply grazed my shoulder. Bill meticulously tore down and packed up the camp. I saw Ellen standing in the distance. She was searching the horizon, in the direction where the Jeep had raced, carrying Ismail. She shouted over to me, her arm pointing at the faraway sky. The line of her finger led to a cloud of black specks of vultures swirling and dipping like mosquitoes over a stagnant pool.

When Bill finished packing the two Land Rovers, we followed the distant shadow of the vultures. The cook was also gone, with all his belongings. Ellen said that when she ran back to the camp on hearing the gunshots, the cook and the other vehicle were missing. We were all silent. My shoulder was burning, and I asked myself why I hadn't tried harder to stop them. They had guns, and they were willing to use them, but . . . What if I had been a different person, able to subdue the kidnappers with the sound of my voice? What if all it took were the right level of voice, the right determination? Instead I had lain at the bottom of that hole, shaking with fear, and comforted by the taste of my own blood, as though that were proof I had tried.

More than once I have come across the heads of my fellow passengers. Most often they were unrecognizable, only fragments—it was only many years of studying anatomy and osteology that allowed me to see them as human heads at all. But some I did recognize. There was the stewardess who spilled coffee on my lap when we hit a pocket of turbulence. There was the large man who grabbed the last copy of *Scientific American* just as I was reaching for it. There was the blown-apart face of the child who sat behind me, constantly kicking at the back of my seat. It floated past me, or maybe I floated past it—it is so hard to tell now who is moving, who is stationary.

When finally we found Ismail's body, it was covered by a black scab of vultures picking at what little meat was left. Ellen jumped out of the Land Rover, a small revolver in her hand, firing into the air. Even when the birds had scattered, she tried to shoot at them, as though the vultures were somehow at fault. When the gun was empty, I saw the tears on her face. None of us had cried up to then. We did not want to admit what had happened, but Ismail's face had been slashed open with a knife and his chest made pulp by countless bullet holes.

Ismail's scream still haunts me. It left me unable to return to Ethiopia. Nor could I continue my research there, or on anything that was connected to that summer. The picture of Ismail's body lying in the hot sun returned to me constantly, the white of the sand become red.

My days passed then in serious contemplation of Ismail's scream. Above me now the blueness of the midday sky is the same sky in Ethiopia under which I had huddled in a ball, terrified, while somewhere I hear parts of me, far off, mumbling. My cowardice and fear left me feeling little more than an animal, something that can no longer think but only grunts and scratches through the day. Was this what Ismail felt when they appeared, guns pointing? Or when they pulled him away, his feet dragging on the old desert? Or when finally they took out knives and slashed open his face and emptied their rifles into his chest? The two of us had had language stripped from our mouths and were left with only antediluvian tongues. As though we were dogs, beaten, our barks become low whimpers.

A year after Ismail's death, I received a package containing a Neanderthal hyoid that had been recently excavated in Spain. The hyoid is a small U-shaped bone that sits behind the jaw, above the larynx and thyroid, and attaches to the tongue. It remains the only articulation we anthropologists have to the beginnings of language. The one shipped to me—small, delicate, resting among layers of rough blue toilet paper and a cocoon of bubble wrap—was the first and only Neanderthal hyoid ever excavated. The excavators themselves were not interested in it, except to note it in their publication, so I had asked if I could be allowed to study it in further detail. Up to that point my career had been spent tracing the evolutionary paths of early hominids. Examining a Neanderthal hyoid presented something of a challenge.

I was searching for something new in any case. After Ethiopia, I found myself growing numb to my previous research, and was reminded of my father, who had searched for a universal language and, later, for all languages. Perhaps a part of me began to understand the reasons for his choices, which up to then had struck me as strange and disturbing, in the years before his death.

The muscle attachments were easy to trace on the rough surface of the bone, and in a cold winter in Michigan, the office heat ever failing, I sat huddled in sweater and overcoat, cramped over the desk, a bright table lamp illuminating the bone's shadowed detail. Following the slight rises and depressions and examining the bone under multiple magnifications allowed me to compare it with human hyoids, and also with chimp and gorilla hyoids. Every point was measured, every angle and distance. A series of statistical analyses of the surface area covered by the various attachments for ligaments and muscles helped me to understand its relationship to the jaw and palate. Ever so slowly, I was beginning to gain a deeper knowledge of the bone, of how it might be related to those first human grunts and mumblings, and I sensed finally I might be unearthing the lowest deposits of language, the first words themselves.

I have come to a decision. I will find the other parts of me. Time has disappeared in this ocean, and ever since those first seconds when my body was all and then diminished, one piece after another has been losing contact, as though the many fragments of myself are disappearing from the radar screen of my consciousness. Each time a fragment vanishes—that sudden moment of loss, as though a limb were cut off—every part shudders. If it does not stop soon, I will lose touch with every part of us, with everything.

A systematic start requires mapping the vectors of the explosion to learn how widely scattered the original wreckage was. I need information on current strengths, on wind speeds, on local storms and weather patterns. I need to know what parts of me are likely to have sunk to the bottom, and what parts are likely still to be floating, bobbing toward some distant shore.

None of this is easy and I tried to employ the aid of dolphins. With their sonar they might easily locate my many scattered selves. But when I get close enough to shout at one, the dolphin approaches, nudges me quizzically, and quickly moves on, having lost all interest. Sea birds are no better. They pick at the scraps of flesh that dot this ocean now, as though it were all a single vast carcass, but remain equally estranged when I call out to them. They take flight, their wings flapping nervously. All this time, I am drifting further and further apart. Soon I will be scattered across the globe. Soon my pleadings will be heard by birds in the Amazon and fish choking in the Thames, by fishermen off the Red Sea coast, by the stone faces on Easter Island. Somebody must hear, somebody must understand.

My colleagues laughed when I first explained my ideas. They thought I was joking. It must have seemed funny at first, strange at least to someone who has not studied the evidence. But the data was unimpeachable and I felt a rising confidence that I could substantially back up my claims with scientific evidence.

It was around this time that Ellen walked in to see me. She

was finishing her PhD, and the frown of concern on her face told me she was both determined and concerned. The work I was doing was crazy, she insisted, it was useless, ever since Ethiopia I had lost it.

How can you possibly hope—she was almost shouting, her hand stabbing the air—to reconstruct a language from a stupid hyoid? If nothing else, what kind of sample size is one hyoid? She looked again as she had that day when she jumped out of the Jeep, her face contorted in loss and anger, the small gun in her fist, firing into the air.

I let her go on. She was worried about her reputation. If it got out—and no doubt it already had—that her advisor was a crackpot, her chances of landing a post would crumble beneath her. I sympathized, but I knew then—as I know even more strongly now—that I was right, my work would be vindicated. If only I could have a chance to present the evidence.

My goal was simply to reassure Ellen, to downplay my claims, to tell her that what she had been hearing were exaggerations, that it wasn't a language I was trying to reconstruct but rather the level of cognitive and linguistic potential. This wasn't true. I had reconstructed the language, but hoped to wait until the opportunity arose to present the evidence to my colleagues in a proper environment. Ellen left, still worried I could tell, although she smiled as she walked out. But she was right. It was Ismail who started it all.

The language I reconstructed was one of grunts and squawks, of deep aspirated vocalizations, of long growls. All this arose from my study of the hyoid, from how the muscles and ligaments had been attached, how the tongue had to have moved. In my office, alone, I practised those sounds, painfully distorting my mouth into shapes that would form such strange and distant voices. In them I detected that ancient sound I heard in Ismail's scream: the sound of an atavistic fear, the fear of *everything*. Alone, at night, making sure no one loitered in nearby corridors, I would let out that scream, as though I too had become a Neanderthal facing something so terrible it defied comprehension. I did not know exactly what it was, but I knew the sound, the scream that gave birth to everything.

This ocean feels endless. The first time I walked out across the badlands in Ethiopia, I believed I had found the meaning of desolation. But I would return to those badlands in a fast second. If only I had been scattered by the vultures, become a fossil myself. Here, amid all this water, I find no part of me that makes sense anymore. Floating past my lower jaw recently, some teeth still intact, it jabbered at me incomprehensibly. The current finally pushed it away, its squawks fading among the growling waves. Now a fear grips me, that when I find the other parts of what is no longer me, none will be comprehensible.

The last I heard of my father was a letter from a neighbour of his in the cramped tenement where he had lived during those final years of his life. It was a brief note telling of my father's death. He had had some last words for me, but the neighbour hadn't understood the language.

I had known he was dying of cancer. I visited him once in those years, when he told me what he had never been able to tell my mother. It had been some years since I had seen him. After my mother left him, he hid from us, refusing ever to give us a current address. All we knew of him were the monthly cheques sent dutifully. Finally, we received a letter from a friend of his, saying he had asked me to come and see him. My mother was not mentioned.

He lay in a confining, single bed in a small one-bedroom apartment in Greenwich Village. There was a pleasant view from the window, and on the roof, he said, was a lush, well-watered garden. The room was full of books—books on Arabic and Swahili, Kazakh and Uzbek, Urdu and Sinhalese, and many, many more. He looked so much older than I remembered. A thick comforter covered his thin body. I made the two of us tea and sat down on a chair by the bed to listen to whatever he wanted to tell me. I had no questions for him.

It was because of the Esperanto classes he and my mother had taken that she left him. She couldn't take his obsession with that crazy language anymore, and one day she packed what she could into three large suitcases and hailed a taxi to her cousin's house in Flushing. My father told me now that she had never understood why he wanted them both to learn Esperanto. It may have seemed a little foolish—especially now that only a few decades after its birth, it was already a dead language—but he had had a reason.

He said that one night, when he was six—perhaps seven, he no longer knew—the whole village was awake, and the night had become a carnival. It was summer, those weeks before the monsoon broke the spell of heat and sweat that made such thick, airless nights. My father didn't know why the people were out. It was no special festival, no holy occasion. Not even the Sikhs in the village seemed to be celebrating any holy day. He went from person to person asking, Why, Babuji? But no one would answer, saying only, Go play with your brothers.

The year, he said, was 1947. The month before, many of his friends had left the village. When India and Pakistan, born as twins, began their sibling rivalry, Muslims were fleeing west across the border while Hindus and Sikhs came east. Those who didn't leave—or were too slow, or were caught (whether at night or in the daytime) on the roads or in the trains—were often killed by whoever was at hand, by whatever weapon was the quickest and most bloody. All the Muslim children he had played with were gone. Where is Sharif? he had asked his mother. Where is Hasan? But she wouldn't answer. Go outside and play now, baccha, was all she said. He had walked over to their houses, but they were deserted. Everything was gone, the doors smashed down, the small fences broken.

Then had come the night that resembled a carnival. Everyone in the village—those that were left, the Hindu and Sikh families—stood in nervous clusters close by the railway tracks that passed through the village. The women brought out sweets and drinks for their husbands and fathers, and the men told jokes, laughed, fell into sudden, uneasy silences. Some were carrying guns, others short blades or kitchen knives, and others just sticks, spears, clubs. The children played war around their parents' feet. My father battled his friend with a twig, shouting loud, pretending he was Arjuna, always victorious.

When he first heard the distant pant of the train, the vibrations resonating along the tracks, there was sudden silence. Somewhere far off, my father heard a voice. Everyone began to move back from the tracks. Someone tugged at his hand, pulling him along, Go home now, go to sleep, they said. But my father stayed, hiding first among all the legs, then behind the tall wheel of a cart.

No lights were on the train that finally approached. Before he could make out anything more than its shadow and the starlight catching the clouds of steam, there was a shattering explosion. The sky lit up, the stars momentarily hidden. The train buckled, was hurled from the tracks. The night filled with screams. The crowd surged forward, waving sticks and knives, guns setting the darkness on fire. My father said he could make out little, could barely see what was happening. All he heard was the screaming, the shouts, the sound— of clubs battering at bodies.

Hours later, in the hot dawn, the ground was a red swamp of blood. Much of the crowd was still there when my father appeared, tired, from his hiding place. There were bodies all around him, beaten, knifed, shot. A hand grabbed at his ankle. He recognized the face—it was the father of one of his friends, a Muslim, who had left the village only a week before. There was a knife wound across his face, and his chest was soaked in blood. My father screamed.

The flight was headed to Delhi when the bomb exploded. It was here, in India, the site of my father's terror, that I was offered an opportunity to fully explain my ideas. A conference on the archaeology of Aryan races and their precursors had accepted my paper on the incipient language of early humans. The topic was only tangentially related, but it was the only meeting that even considered my synopsis. Changing planes at JFK, I thought about my father and that last time I had seen him in his apartment.

In that room, he said that he had once thought Esperanto the only hope. If only people could learn a common language—anything, even Latin, he had laughed hoarsely. He knew he was wrong to have pushed it on my mother. He wished he had told her what he had seen, but he never had. The blood that lapped against the railway tracks was more than he could hope to tell her in any language.

But without a common language, what hope is there? he asked me. I placed my hand on his wrist, surprised to find how little flesh was left. It was almost all bone. With his other hand, he waved weakly around the room, motioning to the piles of books. These past years, he said, I've been trying to learn every language. I thought if the world doesn't learn one, I will learn them all.

I do not know who set the bomb. No doubt some group claimed responsibility. The Tamils or Sikhs or Biharis, or maybe Hezbollah or Kurds or Greek Cypriots or the Red Army Faction or the Libyans or Welsh nationalists or the Basque or Puerto Ricans. It doesn't matter to the dead. I do know I was standing up—I had wanted to get an article out of my briefcase in the overhead compartment. I clicked open the hatch and reached out to prevent anything falling, then searched inside for the handle of my briefcase. That was the last thing I remember. Seconds later I was scattered across the Atlantic Ocean by the force of the blast.

When I told my father that I was studying anthropology at Chicago, that I would soon finish my PhD, and that one day I hoped to lead expeditions in Ethiopia or Kenya, he had smiled. Anthropology, he said, isn't all bad.

I've floated so far out that there is nothing on all sides of me except water and sky. All wreckage from the plane has disappeared from view. Nor do I know how long it has been—days, months, years. I am all alone. I hear no squawks or grunts, only the sound of the waves, sometimes the wind, and I've long since lost hope of finding other parts of me. Some time ago I heard my own voice. I was arguing with my right knee, which had floated by. I desperately wanted to know what part of my body I am, and asked again and again. It soon became clear that we were both saying the same words, exactly the same, yet all I heard were grunts and mumblings carrying an old sensation, a fear in both our voices. As we floated apart, I thought of my father, who had wanted to understand everyone. And those last words of his. Incomprehensible.

The Consul's Wife

ARJUNA LOOKED PEACEFUL, PARVATI THOUGHT, THE WAY HE WAS drowsing, coiled so tightly around the clawed base of the hall lamp. The previous week, when Krishna, Parvati's husband, had told her he was retiring, she had thought of Arjuna, of whether he might like travelling to India. Since then she had studied Arjuna's scales more closely, trying to gauge his moods, his desires, trying to decide whether India would really be the place for him. He seemed so happy here, though, so unperturbed and unperturbing.

He seemed especially happy where he lay, and this made it worse, because she would have to pick him up, this minute. She would have to hide him from the evening's guests. She didn't want to disturb him, to hide him in the hall closet like so many times before. But she knew that if she waited until later, the afternoon, perhaps, or the early evening, it would just be so much more difficult. He would be more lively, harder to control. No, it was better while he drowsed in the morning air. If only Krishna had given her time to prepare the house and dinner. He had managed it before—before he announced the retirement. He was the one to call the caterers, often weeks in advance, the maids, etc. Now it was too late. Next time, she decided, *she* would call the service.

Ever since he said it, that he was leaving the Foreign Service, he had been like this, acting on whims, doing things he would never have done before. Now sometimes he brought her flowers when he came home. Sometimes they drove down the winding coast highway to the Monterey Bay Aquarium and had a long, lethargic dinner at Carmel-by-the-Sea. Parvati found it all very tiresome. She had grown used to his absences, the demands of his work. Now he was like a new child, and she simply didn't have the time or temperament to be a mother again, or even a young bride. And now this round of dinners. Tonight was only the first. He needed to say goodbye—he said, Adieu—to all the men and women he had worked with, the diplomats from other embassies, the officials in the various Federal offices. Only the beginning, thought Parvati, yawning.

She nudged Arjuna, the python, with the point of her stockinged foot, and then bent down and tried more forcibly to wake him. The cool silk of his scales passed across her palms and she found herself instead caressing his silent body, as if paying homage to some deep ancestral memory of her own. Uncoiling him from the lamp, she picked him up, tightly gripping his belly with her slender fingers. He was heavy and bounced like a water-filled rubber inner-tube in her arms.

There was no reaction. Arjuna was dead.

This fact surprised her. Not because she was unaccustomed

to death. Parvati had reached an age where death had become an annual event, and each year she guessed which of her friends and acquaintances would go next. Arjuna had not changed in death. There was no discernible difference from his living self, except that on prodding him roughly, his body only moved as far as her fingers pushed it. It was perverse, she thought, this similarity of life to death. There was not the usual slight shiver which would run the length of his body, a wave, the slightest hint of animation.

Parvati had spent her life following Krishna along the various trajectories of his diplomatic postings. Though she had been born in India and was, by the necessity of her husband's position as a representative of that country, forced to call herself Indian, she no longer felt any attachment to it. It had always been her job, she felt, to assimilate. Her husband was the Indian, the one representing Indian interests abroad. In Spain, while it was natural for him not to learn Spanish, the artifice of the translator allowing for both diplomatic distance and a sense of mutual control, it became equally natural for her to speak it fluently, as though she were a Spanish wife. The same was true in Germany, and later in Japan, though she never did manage to master a fluency in Japanese, however much she tried. With each country, she changed costumes. Though every outfit in her wardrobe carried with it a hint of that old country, that now almost ancestral India, she always tried, as she put it, to go native. She wore kimonos fringed with paisleys embroidered in gold silk, or smart European jackets with diminished collars, hinting at the old Nehru jackets.

Soon they would be going back to India—Back? she questioned—she didn't know what she would do, what she would even wear. This was one transformation her life had not prepared her for. The day he told her, she sank into a shallow depression. Not a deep one. She knew that her position as a diplomatic wife did not allow her to do anything deeply. She sat in her blue funk for two days, barely noticing the comings and goings of her husband, but later, when she thought back to that mood, she couldn't remember what specifically depressed her. There must have been something, she felt, however small, some moment, some sight, some thought. Everything, she felt, was born of a recordable event, however ephemeral. But this mood of hers seemed to have grown either out of something so old she could not remember, or something so new, she had not yet recognized it. She tried not to think about it anymore. In any case, Arjuna was dead. And therefore something had to be done.

The only time she ever saw Arjuna active was when she fed him. Though he was actually Krishna's snake, it fell to Parvati to feed him. Krishna had been given the python, nestled comfortably in a striking, ivory inlaid casket, complete with a manual on care and feeding, by a visiting dignitary, Parvati forgot which country. They all melted into a bland whole of foreignness to her, like the rows of tomato soup cans on supermarket shelves. On the outside of the casket, in bold, handcrafted lettering was inscribed 'Python, family Boidae'. The instructions required that Arjuna be fed on live meat. Small birds, mice, rats, etc. Krishna had no stomach for this. She always considered him one step away from vegetarianism, or worse still, from some brand of Hindu asceticism. She shivered at the prospect.

She enjoyed feeding Arjuna. It was one of the few truly sensual pleasures left to her. There was a large cage she kept outside, one usually used to house rabbits or hamsters, in which she fed him. The mouse inside would bounce from side to side, like a buoy on a rough sea, as she opened the top to drop Arjuna in. The snake would slide down with the ease of a ship dropping anchor in calm waters and squeeze all life from its prey.

Afterwards, she would let Arjuna out and sometimes take him with her into the main dining room. There, slowly stripping away each piece of clothing until she lay naked on the intricately patterned Turkish kilim, she would allow Arjuna to range over her body like the silent breath of an illicit lover. The snake would pass over the wrinkled flesh of her thighs, pushing his way between her legs and then onto her belly and breasts like an advancing infantry accustomed to the shifting undulations of terrain in desert warfare. As the snake's body pressed down on her face, Parvati sometimes lightly pushed out her tongue so that its tip could caress the scales of Arjuna's underbelly. Sometimes she orgasmed, and these were the only times she managed that any more.

Still, she felt no particular attachment to Arjuna except when feeding him, and those rare, sometimes erotic episodes. The dinner party troubled her now. She searched through one of the hall closets upstairs where boxes and boxes of old clothes, long out of use, were stacked. She emptied one. It was packed with kimonos, all different sizes and colours, all for different occasions. In a sudden fury, which came on her quite by surprise, she flung them to the floor, throwing them in all directions before leaving them there, a bright, disordered pile that left her with a feeling of both pride and shame, though the source of neither could she discern. Suppressing her confusion, she took to the matter at hand, which was her snake, and she slid Arjuna into the box as if she were unwinding a long, especially thick length of pasta onto a plate.

Much of the morning had already drifted by and she still hadn't decided what she was going to cook. The light cast by the early sun had disappeared from the living room and was now creeping to the front of the house. A trip to the shops was still required, perhaps even one along the peninsula to purchase necessary ingredients. Parvati fussed nervously in the kitchen, opening and closing cupboards for a clue to the main course.

When Krishna had been posted to San Francisco, Parvati had been delighted. They were both in Indonesia then. He was discussing trade barriers and she was purchasing sarongs, learning about local dishes, watching Gamelan dances, practising her vowels. She had never been to California. But some months after they arrived, she began to feel uncomfortable. There was not a specific manner of dress that she could adopt, there were no specific foods that she needed to learn to cook. When she asked people how she might become more Californian, they often laughed or told her to relax, to mellow out. She did not want to relax or mellow out, she wanted to become Californian.

Instead of searching out what she thought might be the essence of California, the distilled elixir of its blood, she began to think back on her days in India. They seemed so long ago, another life even. She began to think of her childhood as an earlier incarnation. She had lived in a large house, her steps always shadowed by those of servants. Sometimes, when Arjuna ranged over her naked flesh, she remembered she had never seen any snakes when she was growing up. It seemed a little absurd that she came from India and had never seen a single snake. But the servants always killed them or chased them away before they could find her, or her eyes. Sometimes, when she pushed her tongue out until it touched the scales on Arjuna's body, she would think that she had finally caught India, its essence.

Arjuna lay curled on the kitchen table, squashed into a square spiral by the shape of the box. Parvati, pushing the box aside to lay down cookbooks, considered momentarily whether Arjuna was at peace, having entered finally the rain-washed undergrowth of some snake heaven.

Then she had the idea. Arjuna would be the night's dinner. She quivered with excitement as she contemplated it. Was it possible? Would Krishna be angry, or even notice? Would it be bad etiquette to serve a pet to guests? She dismissed these thoughts and concentrated instead on how appropriate a finale it would be to Arjuna's years of service to herself and her husband. What better place to end than on the tongues and in the stomachs of the couple that had fed him with such regularity, such care.

Parvati smiled to herself. She would do it. Already she felt some of that old thrill return, the intoxicating sensation of Arjuna's thick, rounded body mounting her flesh. Goosebumps sprang up in a line along her back.

She had never cooked snake before, nor had she tasted it. She was sure it must taste like chicken. Everything unusual always did. Even if it didn't, everyone was bound to say it did, simply out of politeness. Should she fry Arjuna like a sausage, perhaps garnished with cilantro, she wondered, or stir-fry him in small chunks in a large wok. Was snake-sushi possible? Probably not. She paged through the several weighty books she had pulled down from the shelf above the table. She searched under 'snake' in the index. Nothing. The books were also barren under 'Ophidia' and even under 'Squamata'. There was nothing under reptile. Not a single recipe. This was ridiculous, she thought. She would write to *Good Housekeeping*.

She remembered an eggplant recipe that had turned out tremendously well. It was some Indian thing. She had been cooking Indian dishes more and more lately, having been unable to discover what was Californian in California cuisine. She was sure she still had all the ingredients to flavour the dish. She imagined Arjuna as an extended eggplant, stretched out long and thin on a vegetable torture rack. Her mouth watered at the prospect. Arjuna would be her saviour.

First she had to bake him until the skin turned to a golden crispness, like leaves on a warm autumn day. She placed the snake, coiled peacefully into a spiral, on the largest oven tray she could find. Even then she had to cut off his extremities, which she did with the slow precision of a young woman combing her beloved's hair. When baked, she pulled him out and ran her fingers along the now hot, frangible body. Her nails caught in the brittle scales, which broke off readily like dead bark chipping away from an old tree.

She skinned him next. This proved more difficult than she had expected, as if her longtime-companion was being deliberately recalcitrant. The scales came away easily enough, but much of the skin remained intact, or pulled large portions of the snake's pulpy white meat away with it. She scraped the meat free from these sections and out onto the tiled countertop, poking gingerly from time to time at the small masses of doughy flesh. She half expected them to react, unsure whether some remnant of the life force that had inhabited Arjuna still didn't exist. However, the meat remained motionless and numb to her prodding.

With the skin off, she began to prepare the dish in earnest. Arjuna's insides would be suspended in a thick cream, forming the textured heart of the dish. The dish included fried onions and green chillies, finely chopped garlic, ginger, turmeric and fenugreek seeds, some amchur and a handful of salt.

It seemed perfect. She had not thought about it until now, but having Arjuna for dinner seemed a proper consummation of her own life. She would, in a sense, be returning India to herself. She smiled at this idea. She was not pleased about going back to the real India, but the essence of it she could take. If she could eat it, eat her past in a sense, then perhaps she might start over again, she might be able to become an Indian. It seemed suddenly ludicrous. She becoming an Indian. She laughed out loud. She kissed the decapitated head of Arjuna. Everything smelled so lovely.

Parvati pulled the top from the pan, her face arched high above it so that she would get the full cloud of steam as it rose flavourfully from the cooking. The dish was simmering. It was a striking orange colour, like emergency road signs, she thought.

She couldn't resist. She plunged a finger into the almost blisteringly hot, bubbling mass and pulled it out, flinching from the heat, with a sense of—she wasn't sure what—of victory, of having won a battle? But when she licked her finger, she almost retched and was filled from head to toe with a terrible sense of disappointment. It tasted horribly bitter, Arjuna's stale meat having corrupted the dish, not made it.

She stepped back, staring at the simmering, orange mess. Everything was a mistake. She couldn't remember why exactly she had wanted to cook Arjuna. He had looked so peaceful, dead. She felt tired, exhausted. Her mind felt tired. It was the same way she had felt when Krishna told her they were returning to India, and this morning, when he informed her of the round of upcoming dinners. No difference. It was a stupid idea, she thought. She should have known.

On the table, beside Arjuna's decapitated head, sat the now empty box, and she remembered all the kimonos thrown haphazardly on the floor of the upstairs hall. She had no idea what she would do with them in India. Perhaps she might wear one. There could be no difference, she thought, between herself in Japan and herself in India. In fact, she would wear one that night! Immediately, all the weight of disappointment vanished and she forgot Arjuna and finding him dead and cooking him and how it all turned into a beastly mistake. She would call the caterers right now, she would order platter upon platter of sushi, and she would descend the staircase when the guests arrived, dressed in a kimono. Yes, she determined fiercely, tonight she would be Japanese.

Bodies Motion Sound

I

THE MORNINGS FOUND DAD BALANCED IN A KNOT, BREATHING IN through one nostril and out through the other, sometimes upside down or his feet where his ears should be, and his ears, well, only he knew that. He would walk downstairs stripped to the waist, wearing baggy grey pajamas pulled tight with a cord so that his stomach, when gravity allowed it, swelled like a sack of water over his groin.

He had started yoga when he began peeing in the bed. This was soon after they were married. She was furious with him, but he assured her it was nothing, that with their first child all would be well, and if not with the child, then with yoga for sure. His pissing was the result of the family curse, a legacy of uncontrollable bodily emissions, and one he schemed to cripple through this effort of mind on body and thought on matter. He had warned her when they married, said sooner or later it would begin; his own dad had been a sweater, his body a great cloth of endless perspiration, even in winter his pores would open up, spilling out his essences making his body a mutineer against the season, against the spin of the earth around the sun, against the very nature of bodies and heat and sweat; his grandmother, Mumtaz, was a renowned shitter: her shits could last for hours and on such days her groans travelled all over the house and far down the street; her braying would be incorporated into the games of children, the rhythm of nearby musicians, and the bawdy humour of the young men who lay in wait in the tight alleys of Kampala so they might synchronize their punchline with her outbursts; a great great (and maybe a third great) uncle, Ali, was an endless weeper whose almost ceaseless blubbering started up at the slightest invitation: encountering a sad face, a cloud in the sky, announcements of a wedding or a baby born or dead, a buoyant tune (because it was sure to end), a mournful tune (there, you see), news of deaths in other towns, the first buds of spring: everything elicited for him, if not the immediacy of its sadness or failure, then the promise of such, the knowledge that happiness lay contingent on the dolorous face of daily woe. And there were others: vomiters (like myself), more pissers like Dad, men who ejaculated or women who orgasmed at the slightest provocation, several who lost their hair, grew it back, lost it again, and so on and on; and others: endless spitters and those whose menstrual fluids filled oil drums every month, others whose ear wax erupted in thick strands to be collected in the morning to shape candles; and one, the great and ancient matriarch of this line of shitters and pissers and spewers, evacuators extraordinaire, Razia, whose snot one bright morning remained perched at the end of her nose like a massive and growing fruit, each day enlarging, developing, gaining character and weight, until she could no longer hold her head up and sat with this rock of hardened mucus in her lap until finally it released itself, rolled off her thigh and along and down the hall, rattling doors and windows, scaring animals, scuttling the servants from its path, crashing out through the doors of her zenana and into the world. Reports quickly spread through the town: Razia's elephantine snot had escaped from purdah. Astrologers gathered around it to examine the surface, feel the bumps, smell it, taste it, consider the colour and hardness, and all agreed: the family line was cursed, the snot a wandering snot and the family thus a family of wanderers and disgorgers. Every corner of the world would know them before a child came who, like Razia, produced a globe of snot and, pointing with a finger at a particular indentation, bump or ridge would announce, this is where the family would be allowed to settle in peace.

In the mornings I sat where I could watch him from the kitchen table. When his pants slowly darkened at the groin and urine ran down his legs or spilled over his stomach, cutting slim and transitory rivulets among his whitening chest hairs, I would tighten a fist under the table until my sharp nails pressed into the skin of my palm and turn my head away in disgust. I knew what his face would show: anger and fear. I knew he would untangle himself with an embarrassed awkwardness and stand nervously; under his breath he would curse Idi Amin. He would walk to the bathroom and wash himself. Releasing my fist, I would hope my nails had cut new lines; that the past as well as the future might be changed. I was ashamed of him and hoped that in a new geography of my palm a new family might be written, a new history or a new future. But the skin always flooded with blood and the slight curves where my nails had pressed at the palm faded back into an indifferent brown.

For Dad, it was never the curse of Razia's snot that was the source of our troubles but Idi Amin. They had come to California when they were thrown out of Uganda in 1972 when the Great Bastard, as Dad called him, decided to throw the Indians out. Just like that, Dad would say, cutting the air with a flat hand. Mom was pregnant with me then. She says I was born two weeks premature on a plane, flying from where to where she no longer remembers. I don't believe her. I think she made it up, a way of justifying to herself my rootlessness, the way I skip between fads and fashions, the way I have become so un-Indian.

The Great Bastard menaced my childhood. Dad told me tales of the tortures and humiliations he performed on his subjects, the endless killings and expulsions, and the man himself; no, more than a man, almost an evil god; and the presence of this evil god filled my room at night, enlarging, gorging on the dark, a mammoth and devouring presence that terrified me into performing acts of numb violence on myself: sticking pins into my hand, burning my fingernails with matches, clamping my young nipples in small woodworking vices, allowing young boys to introduce their fingers or their fists into my tender vulva.

Mom and Dad would sit together at night and pray that I

would be the kid who would one day grow that ball of snot; that it would be I who released the family from the curse. They were certain it would be me. Mom says she would shake me angrily, warning me what would happen if I didn't produce that great predestined snot. But I became a vomiter, disappointing their most cherished hopes for my future. I would spew anywhere and everywhere: in the car, at the mall, in the doctor's lap, at school and during phys ed, at birthday parties, when playing with friends or sitting for family portraits. It seemed to stop when I became a teenager, or at least lessen, and my episodes of retching became shorter and less frequent. Dad put it on the yoga. I said never, never. I hated Dad's yoga: having to watch him every morning became only a reminder of his incontinence, a shame I felt far greater than my own. I hated Dad for being descended from Razia, for having me, for the ways our bodies were linked, not only by blood, but by this common stigmata, the way our bodies battled against us and nature.

II

I was nineteen when Mom asked me to teach her to drive. I had just learned I was pregnant and didn't know how to tell her. I didn't know who the father was and probably didn't want to know. I laughed at her when she asked me—I was giddy and afraid—and felt again that old urge, to vomit there and then, to disgorge myself onto the kitchen table like I had done so many times before. 'You drive a car,' I said with a patronizing and questioning inflection drifting into another laugh. I had never thought much of her motor abilities: she was a careless cook, never figured out a remote control, and for minutes after entering a room always cast about, unsure of herself, where to sit, fussing where she might settle her bones with the least fuss.

She stood at the stove making a pot of tea. She frowned at my laugh and confided that she'd already taken lessons with a private company.

I pictured her sitting next to some driver's ed guy, gold chains dangling from his neck. 'You took lessons?' I asked. 'On your own?' and instinctively: 'Does Dad know?'

'Don't tell him,' she said, raising a finger to her lips. 'You know what he will do——fuss fuss about this, that, the insurance, this cost, that cost.'

'Will he let you?' I studied her face closely.

She said nothing. She waited a whole minute, her eyes fixed on the simmering milky tea, and finally offered, 'I don't care what your father says. He can do his silly yoga or whatever, all he wants. You know he never did anything like that in Uganda. He was always saying how silly those holy men in India are. What idiots, he said, and look at him now. Pissing everywhere.' She shook her head feverishly and clamped her lips tight together with an air of disapproval of Dad I had never seen so openly in her.

'Next time you see him,' she said, 'you call him some silly sanyasi and see what he says.'

'I'll call him a fuck if he doesn't.'

She raised a hand ready to slap me but then dropped it, her eyes violent, muttering something in that other language.

I walked out, calling back, 'Whenever you want.'

Our car was a Nissan, smooth and black, and it suited my mood that morning. I was in black: black, leg-hugging jeans, a black tank top and a black leather jacket which I threw casually across the length of the back seat; I had ringed my eyes with black eyeliner, and even my fingernails were painted black; my eyes were hidden behind a pair of black-rimmed Wayfarers. The dash was immaculate, and I threw my small purse with its black eye shadow and nail polish onto it.

Mom nervously jerked the car out of the driveway, her hands tight around the wheel, eyes darting between lanes, right foot pressing the gas. I detected a fragility to her. An arm might crack at any moment, splintering like a dry twig, her leg might come disjointed at the thigh and she would walk always with the strange gait of one whose body no longer suits or fits. I thought of the secret inside me, as if I were possessed of an alchemical mystery, and understood my power. It was a formula that would make her old, make her into a grandmother. The wrinkles on her face multiplied, the bags under her eyes dragged down, and I watched how she laboured slowly with her arms, the sharp jabs of pain from a worsening arthritis, her legs heavy, as though weighted down.

That day in the car it was hot; no clouds in the sky. One of those days when suburbs melt into a bland greyness of concrete and roadway and when you see fat old women by the side of the road, panting, waiting for a bus.

We were on the highway heading west. I remember the

way she looked, wearing large gold hoop earrings glinting in the sunlight, a green Marines T-shirt, I don't know why, and blue polyester pants, and plain sandals with worn tan straps that she insisted were the most comfortable shoes she'd ever worn. It was the first time she'd ever driven on the freeway, and I could see how excited she was. We were in the right lane, and the speedometer wavered between fifty and sixty-five. One of her tapes played in the stereo: Hindi or Urdu or one of those; the soprano wailed like a dying cat.

'Try the next exit,' I suggested. She ignored me.

'Do you see that woman doing her make-up in that car?' Her tongue clicked in judgment. She pointed with a vague gesture but I could see no one. The engine revved faster and the speedometer began arcing toward seventy. It was a busy morning and the freeway, though moving, felt clogged with cars and trucks, as though we were pressing into the diminishing lanes of a country highway.

'What would you do if I was caught shoplifting?'

She laughed. 'I hope you would steal something attractive, not like what you wear.'

'What if I was a heroin dealer?'

'Your cousin was arrested for that,' she said without drama. 'He smuggled heroin and gold.' The freeway opened up ahead of us, and for some distance there were few cars on the road. She slowed down, and I was angry at her for what I guessed was fear of this sudden freedom.

'Who? I didn't know.' Cars began passing us on all sides.

'No one you know. This was when you were a baby.'

'What happened to him?'

'Oh, they hung him, I think. We never found out. He was in Kenya. He was a shitter.'

It was the tone of voice that decided me; the way she said shitter. She said the word with a deliberate hardness, and it was this hardness that I reacted to. There was no rationality in telling her then, no guile on my part, no hope that in a car she wouldn't kill me; there was only myself battering at what I believed was a hardness in her voice, scratching at it, trying to chisel myself into it.

I pulled off the sunglasses and dropped them onto the dash. The thin tube of eyeliner rolled up against them. The sun was now high and the blacktop of the freeway reminded me of the charred underbrush of a field after a wildfire has devoured the surface.

Ahead, a truck laboured up a shallow grade. On its shimmering and silver back doors oversized letters extolled: 'Start the Week out Right. Go to Church on Sunday.' Diesel fumes skated at us over the flat top of the trailer. 'Pass this truck,' I told her. Mom signalled and pulled around on the left. 'Don't brake when you change lanes,' I insisted. She frowned. I was feeling pretty bad. My stomach pushed at my mouth; it wanted to get out right there. The lines of the freeway began to twist and waver. I was no longer sure which lane we were in, or which was the car in front of us.

When I said it, I simply threw it out at her, the way I used to tell her Dad had pissed again or I had lost it on her favourite sari: with short, precise sentences and words, not apologizing or demanding, simply stating. We were back in the right lane, some way ahead of the truck. I closed my eyes and waited. Colours spun around me. I was frightened. I thought she would strike me, throw me out of the car. I could feel the blows already.

After a minute of silence, I felt the car meander briefly, but nothing else, no words or shouts or slaps. The silence was worse, being full of all the blows I was certain were coming.

The car began to slow down. I opened my eyes. Her foot was firmly on the brake. 'What're you doing?' I spat out. She said nothing. Behind us, a truck horn sliced through the air. We were now on a downhill grade and the truck had gathered speed, coming down on top of us.

'Mom!' I shouted. 'We'll have an accident.' But she didn't move her foot. The car stopped with a sudden lurching motion. I heard the sound of air escaping the pressurized brakes of the truck. Its shadow smothered our car, and I thought of the baby inside me and thought I could smell the trucker's breath, stale, stinking of anger.

She was calm. 'Now tell me again,' she said. 'What you just told me.'

The truck's horn erupted behind us, shaking me to my toes.

'Tell me,' Mom said calmly. 'Again.'

Before I could speak, I heard a loud banging from the back of the car. I turned my head and saw the truck driver. He had climbed out of the truck and was thumping his fist on the trunk. I could see his teeth, stained brown, spit spilling onto the back window. He walked around to Mom's side of the car, his fist clenching, unclenching. Cars honked at him. The slow boil of my stomach felt ready to erupt.

'Lady!' he shouted, his voice muted by the thin glass, as though underwater. 'Lady! What the fuck do you think you're doing?'

His eyes terrified me.

She opened the door. The bursting noise of the freeway crowded in on us; the hot afternoon air, the smell of the trucker, of his belligerence, assaulted me. I didn't know what she was doing. She stepped out of the car. I wanted to scream at her to stop, to get back in, to shout for help. But I didn't do any of those. I opened my own door, the hills to my right staggered into mountains and I let my head fall toward the pavement, spewing pale green and white vomit onto the black and insensible surface.

When I sat up I could see her shouting at the guy. Her hands cracked taut gestures in the air; all around us, horns blared, passing cars sucked air from the small cabin, my stomach boiled. This guy was going to throw her into the oncoming traffic. I knew it, and I knew there was nothing I could do about it. I opened my door again and vomited. The puke spilled down the side of the car and formed the beginnings of a channel along the black edge of the highway.

But she didn't die. She stepped back into the car, and for the first time in how long I could not remember, I was filled with a surging pride and love for her. How beautifully she was dressed! How well she looked in that odd T-shirt and cheap pants! The trucker shuffled back to his truck, the car horns and faces now angry with him. I looked over my shoulder as he stepped up into the cab; he looked small and ineffectual, and I thought, how could she have seen that so easily when to me he was a horror.

I searched for something to say; I wanted to tell her how magnificent she had been, how I knew that no one—not Dad, not the kid's father—would have done that for me, but my throat was clogged with vomit and any words that tried to seep out soon choked and were made incomprehensible. I opened my door again and heaved and this time I kept at it for a whole minute, retching and puking, my throat gargling out my innards as though driven by the motor of some impassive engine pushing up against everything I wanted.

When I was sitting up again, I turned to look at her. Her face blistered with rage. Without warning, she started to slap at me violently and I held my arms up weakly to protect myself. Her blows came harder and harder and soon she was using both hands with uncontrolled force. 'You and your father!' she shouted. 'You and your father! To be like that in public. Why can't you control yourself. Always! Always the same!'

When she stopped, my face and arms and shoulders stung with pain. She was crying. I could hear her voice catching in her throat.

'Why do you always have to be sick,' she said.

I said nothing. I could still taste vomit in my mouth. I felt my nose and found it was bleeding. We drove in silence to the next exit where she wound the car around the looped ramp and parked in a 7-Eleven lot. I dropped my head into my hands and felt the warmth of my forehead and the drip of blood onto my bare wrists.

'American girl,' I heard her say. Her voice was rough and excited. 'American girl,' she repeated with a threat in her voice.

I heard the door open and she stepped out and I raised my head and watched her walk into the store. She returned after a couple of minutes carrying a Coke and a handful of paper towels. I could feel my face swelling up already. 'You drink this,' she said without violence. 'It'll settle your stomach.' Her voice was resigned and exhausted. I took the Coke carefully from her hands and drank from the straw. After a minute, I wiped myself clean with the towels. When I examined them, I found less blood than I had expected.

A car pulled up next to ours, its stereo blasting a song by Nirvana that drowned out the music on our tapedeck. Two guys sat in the front. They seemed in no hurry to get out of the car; I could see them joking with each other the way guys do, laughing and punching each other. One turned his head and when he saw me, he winked and smiled. He had a handsome, broad smile and I think the corners of my mouth turned up.

I wanted to say something to Mom, but nothing came, and even if it did I can't now imagine what it might have been because at that moment I had no understanding of her anger: it was an anger not at anything I had done, but at me, at my essence, and there was no way I could persuade her that I was not the person she saw. After a minute, I looked out the window and into the sky. The two guys had walked inside. I didn't want to look at her. I folded my arms on my stomach and pushed hard with my forearms. For a moment I wanted to crush whatever life was inside me. Up in the sky the trail of a plane's exhaust hung like a bridal train. I dug my nails into my palms. I released my arms, though it felt more out of weakness than any decision on my part.

The two guys walked back, each carrying a twelve-pack. Before they stepped inside their car, I quickly stepped out of mine. I could hear her breath release in anger but I slammed the door. I smiled at each one of them and gestured to their car with my eyes. They turned their heads, glancing at each other, surprised, and then they blossomed grins and I got in between them on the wide front seat, feeling the warmth of their thighs squeeze mine. 'Fast,' I said. The car skidded out of there, and the last I saw of her was a figure lost on that small island, waving, as though to a passing plane, the green of her T-shirt burning against the concrete and our black car.

III

I was living with a guy named Bala in a small two-room London flat. Kulwant was already a toddler. I was in Britain illegally and couldn't work and so relied on Bala for food and cash. He was a truck driver who said he came from somewhere east, never telling me where; I thought sometimes that maybe he didn't know, and his curiously olive and brown skin insinuated some mixed Eurasian background. I don't know why he helped me. He wasn't my lover. He had a round of men and women, though I never met any of them. He was a leftie who read Proust and Dostoevsky and picked up strays out of the pricked conscience of what he hinted at were upper-class roots. Those evenings when he was home, which were few, he read aloud long passages from what he called difficult books and then explained them and we would argue because I almost always thought his rendering was half bullshit.

One afternoon he appeared, unshaven, a newspaper folded under his arm and a catlike grin on his face. Inside, he claimed, holding the paper aloft and twisting it in the air, was printed Idi Amin's home phone number. Amin was living in Saudi Arabia, driving a BMW to the beach. A journalist had printed the number in some small leftie paper Bala read; the writer had spent several weeks tracking Idi for an interview, calling him incessantly, following Idi's Beemer, cornering friends, but no luck. Whenever he phoned, a woman answered and said the boss was out. She called him the boss.

Hearing Amin's name resurrected childhood nightmares. I studied the photograph in the newspaper. It was an old one, from his days as dictator. His stare was impenetrable, the stare that had haunted my room at night, the face that had engulfed and menaced my sleep with the certainty that I came from him: without him I would not be who I was, and even as a child I had understood this. I told Bala this, and said that I never really believed in his reality. He was a vampire or a god whose monstrosities were etched in their own hieroglyphic, an unknown language which had for years exerted the influence of its incomprehensible grammar on my life.

Bala urged me to phone. He gave birth to a wicked and becoming smile: 'Go on, call the fucker. He's just another crackpot. You'll be better for it.'

'Maybe,' I offered, 'when you're gone.' He laughed and took Kulwant up in his arms and threw him in the air and caught him with commanding grace. 'Your mum's gonna have a chat with the devil.' Kulwant broached a frightened laugh and I rested myself against a wall, trying not to spew.

I stared at a poster of Malcolm X, one finger pressed against his temple, his face deep in concentration. I liked that poster: it reminded me of Dad doing his yoga, his face serious and without joy. The room smelled musty and was filled with the aroma of old beer and cigarettes. Bala never opened the windows and I never asked him to: he was paying the rent.

I waited until the evening to phone. Bala was out, either driving or getting laid: he never told me which. It was a hot summer night and I had opened the door to let some air in. In the flat above, a party was shifting into high gear. Salsa pounded down through the ceiling and feet beat on the floor in fast, ecstatic rhythm.

Kulwant stood in the doorway, swaying to the music. I didn't know what he was yet: a pisser or shitter or sweater or spewer. After he was born, I cursed him for not having a larger nose, for not snivelling, for not producing snot. Sometimes I shook him violently and shouted into his face, calling him a series of violent and nasty names. But he always smiled back and dribbled and then laughed revealing perfect gums behind thick and fleshy lips and soon I found I couldn't continue abusing him. He could be, after all, no worse than me.

I searched through a battered phone book for the international dialling codes to Saudi Arabia and then found the number Bala had scribbled on a yellow pad that lay among various piles of those books he called difficult, porn magazines and political pamphlets. I picked up the heavy black phone from the floor. It was one of those old phones where you actually dialled every number. The slow process always frustrated me. I carried the phone to the open door. Kulwant pressed himself against my leg. The hall was dark except for light leaking through my neighbour's door frame. From downstairs I heard a woman moaning; I couldn't tell if she was crying or getting laid. I knew who it was: a young Egyptian who had moved in last month. She spoke little English and when I passed her in the hall, she would turn her head away, hiding a bruised lip or a battered eye. She was about my age and when I first spotted her I developed an immediate sympathy for her; she appeared constantly confused, though when I offered help she backed away and shook her head. I never saw the boyfriend or husband, only heard him berating her in a language I didn't know. I told myself that I would do something, but courage always fled me. When it gets bad, I thought, because I didn't know what bad was then. When I told Bala, he would say, 'That bastard. I'll fix him,' but Bala never did anything.

A woman's voice answered the phone. She spoke in a foreign language. For some moments I was speechless. The last thing I had expected was for someone to actually answer. I did not know what to do or say and I realized I had not prepared to answer a real human voice, as though the whole long process of dialling were to me an act in itself; the inevitable exchange was irrelevant.

Finally, I said, 'Mr Idi Amin?'

She said, 'Hold on,' though now with a clear American accent and I was surprised how much those simple words meant to me. I had not heard another American in months.

She came back on the line. 'Who are you?'

I was comforted by her voice and wanted to keep her talking. 'I read the number in that paper and—'

She cut me off. 'You're one of them.'

'No,' I said, and oddly, I found myself wanting her to be on my side. 'It's not like that.' But I didn't know what it was like. I didn't know what I wanted to say.

Her tone softened: 'You're an American?'

'Sort of.'

I heard a muffled laugh of understanding. Then from somewhere behind her I heard a voice. It was a man shouting. A deep, bellowing voice calling out in a language I didn't know.

'Hold on,' she said again, but this time with greater intimacy.

I heard the two of them shouting at each other, and after that her voice again. 'You didn't really want to talk to the boss, did you?'

'I don't know,' I said honestly.

'There've been so many like you these last few days. They call for what reason? I don't get it. He's just a fat old motherfucker. You should know this. That's all he is.'

'But . . .' I stopped.

'I don't know your story but this isn't the guy you want. Not anymore. Why not just let the fucker die?'

'I didn't know he lived.'

There was silence after that. Then I heard the phone being placed onto a hard surface and I heard voices again, now quieter.

Then someone picked up the phone and said something with a thick, gruff voice, the kind of voice I imagined a crabby but well-meaning grandfather would have. I said nothing. Then the voice again. It was more demanding now. I didn't understand the language. It was not the voice I had expected. It was a man's voice, and somewhere behind him I heard a woman's subdued laugh. Was that all he was?

Finally I said what I'd meant to say all along, only I hadn't realized until that moment.

'You great bastard. That's what my papa calls you. The Great Bastard. I think he's too nice.'

There was a long silence, then shouting, and finally I dropped the receiver back into the cradle. My hands were shaking.

Downstairs the moaning had travelled out into the hall and I forgot for a moment about Amin and stepped outside to see what was happening. The young Egyptian woman sat on the landing below, squatting against a wall. She was bleeding from a cut slicing down from one eye. Her small body heaved back and forth as she let out low groans of pain and anger. I picked Kulwant up. I could hear a man shouting from inside their apartment and I resolved to go down there immediately. But as I carried Kulwant back inside, I doubled over and fell. Kulwant slipped from my hands and I began to throw up more violently than I had ever done before. I heaved and retched and spat. My insides felt like they were being ripped right out of me. I was on the floor for a good five minutes and a thick pool of my own vomit formed around my hands and knees. Kulwant stood a few feet away, staring at me and grinning.

I turned over and lay on my back. Sick was everywhere. Floating in it were porn magazines and difficult books and political pamphlets and the phone and what few clothes Bala and I owned and Kulwant's toys and I looked up at the ceiling and breathed in something of my own stink. The music from the party continued to pulse through the walls and I heard Kulwant's laugh and I looked across at the door to discover him in the arms of the young Egyptian woman. She balanced him with one arm and stood impassively, staring at me with a mixture of curiosity and bewilderment and unabashed need. I could tell she had no idea what to do. I held out my hand so she could help me to my feet. A line of red arced down her cheek. I told her I'd clean the cut up and bandage it. She handed me Kulwant and he giggled as he was passed into my arms and I saw something I had never seen before: the faces of my parents shining in his features. The image lasted only a moment, and then it was gone. I wondered if I was softening.

I led the Egyptian woman to the bathroom. It was down the hall and on the left. Inside, with the door shut, the music was muffled. The mirror was decades old and the backing silver half gone. The only way to get a clear picture of myself was to keep moving.

The Order of Things

It's only a game, he shouted, voice fading on the wind. Those very words. I could still feel the grip of his fingers where he had held my child's arm, his hand large, engulfing it, fingers touching at the tips. A line of grey already infected his beard, though a young man, yet even then retired and a national name. His beard tied back into a second, scruffy chin, a pink turban, his eyes on me, Watch the ball, not me, and again his voice, Watch the ball! But I always looked back into his eyes. Why was he here, why wasn't he out there, where the newspapermen attacked each other for his photograph, where the radio sang his praises, where all India looked to the holy dirt his feet walked on? It's only a game, he shouted. They said he had walked with Gandhiji to the sea. They said that he never, not even as a baby, wore anything but homespun. They said that on every corner he passed, an assassin waited—why?—but that divine forces protected him. I launched the cricket ball into the air, and it fell thudding in the hot dirt only a few feet away, a red, undistinguished ball, and he looked at me as though I, personally, had lost Pakistan.

Over thirty years later they found his body in one of the small alleys suffocating the dark streets around the Golden Temple of the Sikhs, the shops crowding into it, the hands of beggars having stripped most possessions from his body, a kirpan, a holy knife, in his gut. I heard this on the BBC World Service, sitting alone—my wife had taken our daughter shopping for a prom dress—in our Berkeley home with its fake English countryside façade. Outside, the automated sprinklers silent in the drought. That year, the lawn died as summer aged. Three days ago, and only now had the news squeezed out of a Punjab under martial law. A month before, Indira Gandhi's own Sikh bodyguards had murdered her, claiming it as vengeance for the attack she had ordered some months previous on the Golden Temple. Thousands had been killed in that original attack, and thousands more died after the assassination. Anil was Kirpal's son and my business partner and he celebrated both events, because both, he assured, would show the Sikhs how important it was to have a separate country, to finally rise up and forge a free Khalistan.

But why hadn't Anil told me of his father's death? I had spoken to him two days before and he had said nothing. I pressed the button on my phone with his name on it. Anil? Anil, I heard, I . . . I don't know what to say . . . His voice, clear, strong, Yes, yes, I know, the falling sari prices in Pakistan. Have you seen *The Wall Street Journal*? What? I said, confused. No, Anil bhai, I heard about your father. Kirpalji. Your father. It is terrible news. I am so sorry. And then, my voice revealing a strained but rising frustration, Why didn't you call and tell me, why did I have to hear this on the radio? Anil was silent, and I could imagine him looking at the telephone, annoyed. He was never one to talk about things like this, never one to give reasons, root out explanations. Finally he said, The funeral was yesterday. They took his ashes and dumped them in the Ganges. His wish, and not the Sutlej as we wanted. For all he did, he was at least a hero of Punjab. They should have thrown his ashes in the Sutlej. Then he added, his voice crisp, unaffected, We are still on for the auction tomorrow? It is important with all that has happened. But I protested, Anil, we don't have to do this, we don't, you know.

Anil merely said, You know Papaji and I, we had our differences.

The dying lawn, fading into dusk, and I thought of my father's house in India, in Punjab, standing next to Kirpal's with its constant guards. Our small, cramped rooms leaked out onto roads of dust, fields of dirt. How far we had come in so few years.

Both houses looked out onto a large square of dirt, where every now and then, tents blossomed overnight like mushrooms, heralding the sudden animation, the music, the air of licence and possibility of a wedding celebration. At other times, we kids played in the square, kicking up dirt, running, a kite string threading through my fingers, the paper kite behind me, rising until it was almost gone, smaller than the sun, and I would pull it in, afraid it might disappear. Anil, eyeing the dead kite, a lazing bird, feathers ruffled by the breeze, would shout at me, Why did you stop? Why did you pull it down? His face angry, as though my fear had lost him that world up in the sky where he could look down and see his father only as a dot, growing smaller and smaller.

Those days, my legs stuffed into trousers, a white cricketer's shirt, and Anil the same, his fingers pulling at the collar, Papaji, it's so hot, and Kirpal saying, This is how real cricketers play. And on the far edge of the field, the kids we always played with, dressed in torn shirts, no shoes, we envious of their freedom, they awed by the shadow of the great man, too timid to approach. They said he argued with Nehru over Partition. They said his voice rang out in fury when Jinnah announced, a day early, the formation of Pakistan, casting the shadow of a split land onto the fireworks, the celebrations of India's birth, because, they said, Kirpal didn't care whether the British stayed or left, all he wanted was India whole. Nehru's ears rang with his abuse, Why do you let Jinnah split up the land? Why do you let them take a knife to our Punjab? But to us he was the memory of fame, that arc of muscled arm, that streak of red through the sky, toppled wickets, victory.

Kirpal's thick fingers enclosed my arm, holding it just right, forcing my hand around the red ball, hard enough to kill a man. Like this, no, like this, he said, his fingers pushing my hand into impossible positions. Cricket is a dance of the hand and you must learn the moves precisely, that's it, yes, that's right. I would throw the ball, watching it skid far off in a momentary breath of dirt pulsing up from the ground. His shout, Anil, get the ball! And Anil would run, faltering, his father's voice, Quickly, quickly, my arm still hurting from where he had gripped it, where his fingers pressed into the soft flesh. And Anil, standing, his eyes on the ground, in the distance the kids watching, a kite on the ground, unmoving,

Come on, boy, that's it, hold the ball, just so, no, not like that, here, put your arm like this, here, bend your elbow when you bring it back up, keep the wrist loose, no, Anil, not like that at all, you're holding the ball like a girl, hold it like a man, you can't always throw underarm, a man, Anil, do you know what a man is? Do you know what a Sikh man is? Come on, hold it properly, who formed the Khalsa? Do you know why? Anil! Hold the ball like a man, properly, no, I'm not hurting you, I'm only showing you how to, Anil! Okay, go inside, go sulk, be a girl! And the great man watched his son kick up dirt, hands on the tight collar, his eyes on the ground. Now, Raj, again, but keep your wrist more loose when you run, yes, that's it, great! I threw the ball as hard and fast and straight as I could and watched it bounce some distance off, the red of it fading. I knew, even then, that if I were a real friend to Anil, I would have dropped that ball at Kirpal's feet, I would have walked away, my hand fingering my collar, my feet kicking at the dirt. But this was Kirpal, the dying sun behind him, and even so young, we had our gods.

Anil double parked his orange Mercedes outside my store in Berkeley, one hand pressing on the horn, the other waving at me, his lips moving, Hurry up! Hurry up! It was a busy morning, the students filling the sidewalks with their bodies, their nervous, urgent energy, and I, not even finished with my first cup of tea and already in the middle of a big sale, and then Anil, the horn blaring, the arm waving. Neema! I called out to my wife. Neema, Anil bhai is waiting, and I still haven't finished with Mr Sheik. I smiled at Mr Sheik. Neema, please finish with Mr Sheik, and to Mr Sheik, thin, balding, though young, eyes alive, I said, My dear wife will conclude the sale if you do not mind. My business partner is impatient this morning. Mr Sheik nodded, Yes, he said, Please to tell we are all sorry for his loss. Yes, yes, of course, gathering up my briefcase, the horn blaring, and Neema, Don't forget your jacket. Of course I get it, but she is frowning, her eyes not on Mr Sheik, an important customer, but on the orange Mercedes, orange, the national colour of Khalistan, her tongue nervous, Give him my best, and say I will call Anita this evening. I nod. The street, treacherous with students. Why the hurry? But the car is already swerving onto University Avenue, and Anil, his face dense, illuminating nothing, says only, These bloody hippies, If I could kill one . . .

Anil is a short man, strong, broad shouldered and muscular, hair creeping down the sides of his neck. Ever since those days of playing cricket, he has grown to the sides and not up, building layer upon layer of muscle, fat, as though preserving that self he was as a child, kicking up the dirt, his eyes down, the cricket sweater tight, hot, the collar suffocating. Before he started wearing a turban, his hair was already thinning, greying, and his hands, when we sat together some evenings, a bottle of Johnnie Walker between us on the table, his hands would find his head, straightening, covering up those first signs, not wanting to admit that one day his hair would be like his father's.

I didn't know what to say, so I said, quietly, Anil bhai,

searching for traces of grief in his profile, but all I found was the hard shell of something else. Anil bhai, I am so sorry. Neema too. Mr Sheik even. He shook his head. At a light, he pressed his hand on my arm, and briefly, he glanced over at me. Do not say anything. I know. It is not easy, but work must go on. I said to Anita this morning. Anita, I need to work, without work, what am I? And she still crying. Did I cry? No, he was an old man, and old men die. The car lurched forward, his hand on the stick again, and then he burst out, Bloody hippies! A young woman dressed in tie-dye, her long hair flowing, walking in the street, casually, and Anil had to swerve to miss her. That was why I was late this morning, he shouted, because of gora hippies like that one! They parked me in, some VW with stickers all over it. The Grateful Dead, and all that whatnot your daughter listens to. Next time . . . But he broke off. We were on the freeway, and his foot went to the floor as the car menaced across four lanes, the horn suddenly blaring at someone who tried to cut us off. I had never seen him drive like this, overtaking without giving cars a chance to get out of the way, or if this was impossible, flashing his lights, pressing the horn, Come on! Come on! What are you doing, you stupid woman! Go back to Mexico! Berkeley became Oakland, its long stretches, dead tyres rolling between lanes, sixty, seventy, eighty . . .

Over twenty years ago, our parents waved to us from the dock, their small figures submerged in the crowd, until eventually, we couldn't distinguish between the families and the whole dock, those thousands of faces, merged into the grey horizon that kept us looking back to India, enchanting us with its memory of stillness. When we approached the United States, for several minutes we had the illusion of returning, but this disappeared when we saw the hubbub on the dock, the skyscrapers behind it, and no one there, waving to us. We started a business in Berkeley, and in a few years, our small import-export storefront had expanded so fast that soon we controlled much of the sari trade on the West Coast, and even parts of Canada. Our parents found us wives, and we flew back for the wedding, nervous, laughing, smuggling Johnnie Walker in our luggage, all the time talking boldly of what we would do that first night as men.

Anil, come here, son, he said. I stood watching, hours after the wedding. He looked so much older, the grey in his beard having expanded like a fungus, eyes tired. He hugged Anil, his broad chest pressing his son close. Now you are married, and Anita such a fine girl, with a degree and everything, just like you wanted. The old man beamed. Anil, his body limp in his father's arms, already strong, stocky, no turban yet, pushed Kirpal away, though gently, without force. Thank you, he said formally. And Kirpal again, Now I am in the government, you know, I hope you do well to my name abroad. I am more important than ever. I have meetings with our dear Indira almost every day. Indira! snorted Anil. She is a . . . But he stopped himself, and I could see the red rise to his face. Sorry, but I don't share your politics, Father. Anil moved back, turned, and quickly pushed out through the tent which stood on that old field where we had practised cricket until our arms hurt and our knees ached. I thought I saw in his retreating figure something of the boy pacing away, angry. But he was a man now, and there was nothing Kirpal could shout at him. Kirpal stood alone, suddenly ancient, his shoulders slumped, his eyes looking down at the dirt, one foot etching a circle. If there had been a cricket ball in sight, I would have picked it up, running, my arms and hands perfect, the arc of that ball, just to show that after all these years I had not forgotten who he once was. But there wasn't, so I said, Sat Sri Akal, bowing slightly, and followed Anil, nervous, thinking, Neema is more beautiful than in the photographs, but I hope she doesn't want too many babies.

The 1980s closed around his neck like a noose, those years before his murder, when the rumours began to surface. Slowly at first, like the dead bodies on the side of the road, those rare births of night, first a Hindu, an old man, then two nights later, a pair of Sikh brothers, then a Hindu family in a neighbouring village, then . . . The rumours expanded in the heat of the worsening trouble, when so many years had gone by and all Kirpal wanted was the mantle of the old statesman, the dignified aspect of his beard, one shake of the hand and the deal done. He felt forced to give a speech against the separatists, against the widening cycles of violence. Punjab must never become Khalistan, thumping his fist on the armrest of the chair, his face on every television. India must remain whole, though wounded, having already lost its pound of flesh in 1947. The radicals were murderers, arsonists, nothing more than petty criminals and terrorists. The police must be given full authority to quell these troublemakers. I did not walk with the Mahatma to see our country come to this. His face lost in nostalgia. I watched the videotape he sent Anil of the speech, specially copied to play on an American VCR, only to sit as Anil frowned, grinding his teeth. The old fool, he doesn't know history when he sees it, Khalistan will overrun him. But watching Kirpal's face on television filled me with an old feeling, and I remembered I had always thought of him as my father, the one who made it possible for me to come to the States. But to Anil I said, You're right, the old fool. And it felt right.

It was only a month after this speech that Indira ordered the attack on the temple, and it was Kirpal, so rumour had it, who pressed her to rout the fighters from our holy shrine.

But other rumours were already being passed by whispers. They said reporters started them, always pushing their noses in, but others that someone in the government, in his ministry itself, an internal power struggle after the attack on the temple, a hand that forged originals, changed the past, but others that CIA was involved, or even KGB—they all knew his hatred for communists. No one could prove anything. They said, wasn't it strange he retired from cricket in 1947, at the height of his career? They said, but this was only a rumour of a rumour, that he refused to play for a free India, that he only ever played for the glory of the Raj. They said, laughing, the old man wants the British back. Why not send him over there, retire him with an OBE? There were photographs from the forties—him, no turban, on his knees to some white sahib, his lips approaching the feet—and this on the front pages of all the rags. And then they said he never marched with Gandhiji at all—he was playing a match in

Trinidad. Where were his loyalties in 1947? Was his argument with Nehru only a speech he gave attacking Nehru, attacking the bloody passage of independence? And where were his loyalties now? Why did he attack the separatists when everyone knew what his son was up to? The old man's hand in every pot, his fingers dirty.

They made him resign, made him leave the humiliations of Delhi and return to his Punjab under martial law. Arthritis in his joints, feet shuffling from the house, across that old square field, barely the strength to kick up any dirt, walking to the bomb-scarred and shattered walls of the temple. They said he sat for hours in prayer, often overnight on the cold stone of the Golden Temple, his eyes on the water of the temple pool. Anil said it was better this way, better he was out of politics, even though he still gave speeches, still attacked the separatists. It gives me a free hand, no more of his damn meddling, always messing things up. Do you know, but . . . I had stopped listening, knowing this was not the way it should be. An old world, an old nostalgia had been laid bare, battered, dead. Those ancient gods had vanished, and all I wanted, middle-aged, was an order that would assure me, tell me who I was, now, so far away.

It was during these years that Anil started wearing a turban, attending gurdwara regularly, a kara on his wrist, a painting of Guru Govind Singh garlanded in the living room, and a kirpan, the sheath studded with jewels, hanging over his desk. Often, when I needed him, he was gone, his secretary smiling, Sat Sri Akal, Mr Gill Singh, Anil Singh is at the gurdwara, so please to wait because he will be back soon. At the gurdwara at two in the afternoon? I would ask sometimes, and she would smile, nod happily, Yes, of course, Mr Gill Singh, your partner is very devoted these days, and her secure voice would intone, Wah Guruji. On the wall a calendar showed Hindu atrocities against the Sikhs. This month a man lay in a pool of blood, an old man, his body riddled with bullets, and somewhere in the shadows, where the camera lens could barely focus, a woman caught in her sudden grief.

At the sari auction, all deals went to us. It was a large cold hall with makeshift chairs and tables set up informally, everything hopelessly confused. Bidders wandered for minutes, unable to find where to sign in. Anil watched smiling, his eyes on the eyes of others, searching for what they were looking for. He was a master at these auctions, his instincts exact, knowing when to let off bidding, certain always when no one would challenge his last bid, when to give in and allow something to go to another determined hand. But this day he never gave in. Everything he wanted, he got. I don't know if it was out of respect for his father, or because Anil looked exceptionally fierce, unstoppable, something burning inside him, but no one challenged him for long, their hands fading from exhaustion. That day, Anil made for us the greatest deals of our lives. It was something to watch.

Hands slapped him on the back, others hugged him nervously. Sat Sri Akal, we are all so sorry to hear, Parvati, she says, Oh, what a great man Kirpalji was, oh, what a great man. And others, Wah Guruji, So terrible, not only a personal loss but a loss to the country, and the way he died, oh, oh, oh. Such a pity. Anil backed away from the hands and the long lines of condolences, many mixed with a look of awed respect at how much he had made in a single day. His eyes no longer searched through the room, guessing at tactics, but drew into themselves, in what appeared to be remorse, almost grief. There were other voices, ones I heard but I doubt Anil did. Shhh, not here, the ashes still warm . . . All his money goes to them to buy . . . I caught the conspiratorial nod that ended the sentence. Still others, voices lowered, my own hearing heightened. They say it was he who gave the stories to the papers, those stories that brought him down. The disgrace, the shame of him. I told Anil that we should be leaving now, that Neema was swamped back at the store, and there was no one else to help today. As we walked out, eyes on us, I felt uncomfortable, even though I was among so many familiar faces, as though I too had played a part in Kirpal's death.

My father was a communist. Not the modern type, the failed type now eulogized on CNN. He was a successful communist, as far as one can exist. He was the old sort, the intellectual who read Marx and Engels, had in his youth modelled himself after Trotsky, and even after Stalin's betrayal, could find no stain on the body of the Soviet Union. His world was one of ideals, of possibilities, but also one of a genial pragmatism. It was not my world. I never saw any sense in equality. What could equal Kirpal's arm as it bowled one of his famous fastballs? Why did the neighbourhood kids always stand in awe of Kirpal, afraid to approach? These were elemental questions my father's politics could never solve. When Kirpal was elected to the National Assembly on the Congress ticket, my father saw no contradiction in walking across to his neighbour's house with a plate full of freshly made laddoos to celebrate the victory. I never forgave him for that, to bring Kirpal down, to make him an equal.

But still, he was a communist, and with that went regular raids, occasional imprisonments, sometimes even of guests, his papers searched through, and once, Neema's letters, the letters of his new daughter-in-law were confiscated, examined for potential subversion, and to this day rot in some file in Delhi. When my father died, he died broken hearted, recently returned from jail and countless rounds of humiliating questions and beatings. Kirpal wrote to tell me how sorry he was for my father's death, and that—and here the pen wavered slightly on the paper—it was he as Home Minister who had ordered the raids, the persecutions that had slowly withered my father's heart, finally eroding his faith in all politics, until, in his last days, all I am told he did was watch cricket, the red ball arcing through the air, the wickets flying, a place finally where he could find grace and justice. I didn't feel resentment or anger against Kirpal when he wrote to tell me this. I don't even know if I still have the letter. It was necessary. In those days, everything seemed necessary, reasonable. It made sense to me, and strangely, it revived my faith in my father, restoring him to an order he had always sought to break. I sympathized with Kirpal's anguish and was shocked to find Neema so angry, almost screaming, when I showed her the letter. He was a communist after all.

We sped away from the auction, Anil driving faster now than before, as though possessed of some need to get away as quickly as possible, to escape those voices offering condolences and congratulations in the same breath. On the freeway, he pressed the horn at the slightest provocation, at people fifty metres ahead changing into our lane, or at a car going seventy-five in the fast lane. I was nervous now, though not about an accident, because I began to sense something else in Anil's face, in his almost maniacal driving. I felt, strangely, that there could be no accident. The accident had already occurred, and that's what gave Anil the courage to drive like this. My nervousness grew, ballooning, almost reliving the accident that hadn't happened, spinning, tumbling over and over. Soon we were already on the streets of Berkeley and Anil's driving was no better. Ahead of us, an old black woman crossed against a green light, and I was jolted by the car horn, somehow more insistent than before. Anil didn't slow down, though now the woman was out of our lane. The horn blared on, Anil shifted the wheel, pointing the car at the woman, and we headed for her, though she refused to acknowledge the screaming horn, the screeching brakes. The car spun out of control at the intersection. The seatbelt ripped into my chest as my body rushed forward, Anil swearing beside me. We came to a stop, all turned around, facing the oncoming traffic, horns blaring around us, the old woman still ambling away, ignoring the commotion, Anil's yells, You bitch, you bloody bitch!

In those years of Kirpal's waning influence, as the rumours gathered around him like a mist that no power seemed able to dissipate, that led him, blind, to his murder, Anil, they said, was seen in the company of certain men. I never asked him about this. It was none of my business whether his share of the profits went to help finance the separatists, to lay the foundations of a civil war. Even before the rumours began to strangle Kirpal, before the separatists became a threat to the fabric of India, Anil, they said, was sending them money. And later, when the temple was attacked and those thousands killed, and Anil stormed into my shop, I could read on his face a mood caught between the poles of emotion, a grand anger against Indira Gandhi for what she had done, yet a joy also, for he carried a newspaper which he waved like a flag and shouted, The war is here, clapping his hands together like a magician. I looked at him. Neema stood behind the counter and shook her head. I knew she was going to shout at him, and so I had to stop her. Anil, I said, what are you talking about? This is the temple they attacked, what is there to celebrate? But he laughed, Come with me, we should go meet some men I know, and I was already following him when I glanced back to Neema and saw anger and reproach in her eyes rising like dust on an old field. Neema said nothing, and I stood there, unable to move, and prayed for someone to tell me what to do, because all I wanted was to know who I was in this world and where my place ought to be. I stood paralyzed, waiting for something to happen, for someone to do something. Nothing happened. Anil only laughed again and walked out as though there was no question in his eyes where I stood, and it was some months later that I heard on the radio of Kirpal's death, and I thought again of

Anil's laugh that day and of myself, standing, as though I was a child waiting for Kirpal to throw me a ball. When Anil walked out, he no longer walked with a child's self-conscious gait, and I remember this because I searched for something familiar in his retreating form and I found nothing that I knew.

Many people sent them money. We all knew that. Many were proud of it, and I wouldn't take anything from that pride, well deserved if they were doing something for a cause they believed in. I did not finance the separatists, and neither did I speak out against Khalistan. I still remember that look of anger on Kirpal's face, that look of defeat when I threw the ball and it landed only a few feet away, a look which said that it was this sort of failure, this specific lack of effort, that had allowed India to be split up. I don't know if this is true. All I know is that all those around me—my father, Kirpal, Anil—they all seemed reasonable and honest men.

The car wasn't seriously damaged and we were able to drive away before the police arrived. Anil was silent, no more swearing, and when he dropped me off at the store, he told me not to worry. With all we did today, Punjab will soon be free, a Sikh state. I placed my hand lightly on his lap and stepped out of the car feeling empty and exhausted. My heart was beating fast. The street was less crowded now, though a young man in torn jeans, no shirt, long blond and knotted hair took a meandering path toward me. I stopped. I don't know why. I thought for some strange reason he was going to hit me, and that if he did, it would be right because that was the order of things.

Border Song

Bikram sang. Usually old Punjabi or Hindi movie tunes, but her repertoire had expanded since moving to California. She had learned the theme to *M.A.S.H.* and all the songs on Abba's *Greatest Hits Volume One*. She sang all the time. Her voice echoed the rhythm of frogs that had invaded her childhood nights with their persistent croaking. She filled up the spaces of the house with her songs, and she let her songs breathe outside—in the garden, in the busy, cramped aisles at the Safeway, during those hours she spent alone, when everyone was out, gone to work or to school. Song was the gold jewellery she had carried with her from one country to another, across freshly painted borders. Now it seemed an heirloom, an artifact excavated from a lost world.

Ravi, her nephew, believed when he was young that she sang solely for him. Her voice was high and sharp and full of force and energy and belied her small, self-effacing frame, always covered with an old silk sari and one of the many jackets Harbans brought back for her from the store. These were 49ers, or *Charlie's Angels*, or The Who tour jackets, all promos, all sent gratis to one of Harbans' several convenience stores. Bikram almost never spoke. She expressed herself through her songs, and only reverted to English or Punjabi, or more likely a mixture, when a song couldn't say it.

Years later, when Ravi was older, he would see how she always sang, or hummed, or muttered to herself, and it seemed a betrayal. It wasn't for him, it never had been, and his aunt wasn't a private songster. She was defective, he later concluded, her voice the manifestation of a person unhinged or askew.

The only time she stopped singing was to tell a story, and at such times she seemed to take substance before Ravi's eyes, even gaining weight. His own mother never told stories, she worked late and was always gone when he fell asleep, often to the thickening night of his aunt's voice. Speaking changed his aunt's body. Her lips struggled against the words, as if trying to sing, to reform story into melody, and her voice, far from songlike, shuddered as if disturbed by the strange junctures that existed in speech. A word became unreal on her tongue and only lost this weight of speech when connected to a tune, when it would merge into the next word of the song.

Every story was different, mutated from the previous version, as if she had a horror of repetition. A leopard in one tale became a frog in another, a slighted crow transformed into the antagonist in the next. In one, an alligator ate the bird, in the following, the bird, like a snake, unhinged its jaw and swallowed the writhing, snapping form of the alligator, right down to the struggling tail. Ravi was never disappointed by these inconsistencies, and showed no surprise at the transubstantiation of mouse into elephant or tiger into hyena. They were no more curious than a mad aunt who sang, and one, sane, who told stories.

One day, Bikram told the story of the dying king and his three children.

The old king knew he was dying, and was unsure whom among his three children, two sons and a daughter, would succeed him. He decided to hold a contest. He gave each child one hundred pieces of gold, and the one who filled the hundred rooms and the great hall of the palace completely using only this money would be the future ruler.

The eldest son took off immediately to the market, certain of his success. He spent the money on sacks of coal and soon a procession of donkey carts meandered up the hill toward the palace gates. But the unloaded coal barely filled a quarter of the great hall, and left the remaining rooms deserted—and the mess it made took several days to clean up.

The second eldest, the other son, laughed at his brother's idiocy. He also walked down the hill to the market where he spent his one hundred gold coins on something sure to fill every room of the palace from top to bottom—sacks of wool! The procession that now found its way up to the palace was like none that had ever been witnessed before. Indeed, when the first carts arrived, the last had not yet left and for some hours the road was a single organism of donkey carts wending their way ever upwards. But even all this wool, flung loosely through open doors and windows, barely filled the great hall, while the remainder, all those rooms and chambers, stood starkly empty. To the king's annoyance, tufts of wool were being pulled from the carpets and chairs and tapestries for months after.

The youngest, the daughter, remained slumped in contemplation of her brothers' mistakes for several weeks, silent, then without warning, disappeared, taking the gold with her. She was gone for many months, leaving the old king despondent, thinking she had given up and was living in a distant land, frittering away the gold pieces one at a time. The brothers scorned her, believing now they would share the kingdom between themselves. Then one day, after many months, the daughter reappeared, climbing the hill, and a procession of one hundred men and women followed. This was all she could muster, the brothers scoffed. Surely they had won the kingdom now! The daughter placed a single man or woman in each of the hundred rooms of the palace, and placed herself in the centre of the great hall, and while the old king watched with surprise, she began to sing. The song spread from room to room, and soon the whole palace was filled with their voices. For she had travelled the countryside searching for the greatest singers in the land, and as the song stretched into the night, the old king died, and the first queen of the land took her throne.

It was in 1964 that Bikram and Harbans left India and moved to California. Bikram didn't know why they moved, nor did she care much, but then, as a new bride and one who had presented so many difficulties during the search for a husband, she was told not to ask. For two years they lived in Oakland, by Lake Merritt. She could see the lake from the single window of their apartment. In the summer, sunsets glistened red and orange and sometimes pink. Harbans spent his days out. He was trying to start a business, though he never told her what kind. He was continually having 'meetings' and 'discussions', and promised they would soon be 'in the money'. Every day, Bikram walked two blocks to the grocery store where she could find nothing she wanted to buy and so bought everything she didn't want. Once, she walked out to the lake but found people stared at her in her sari, and when she looked down at the water, it was streaked with gasoline and oil and on the surface cola bottles and tin cans bobbed like dead fish.

Soon after Harbans said they were 'in the money', they moved away from Oakland and into the hills where there were still few houses. Bikram could no longer walk to the grocery but had to rely on Harbans or travel with him on Saturdays. It was only years later that she learned to drive, thanks to her sister-in-law, Jyoti, who had come from England after her husband died. Jyoti had two children, Ravi and Meena, and Harbans reluctantly offered them a home.

Before this unexpected arrival, the house remained unfurnished. No money yet, not for furniture, said Harbans. Bikram filled the rooms with her voice, roaming from one empty room to the next, singing or telling stories to herself. A single step led from the hallway to the living room, and this single step struck her as a great luxury. She would sit on it for hours at a time, staring at the far blank wall, standing only so as to relish the joy of once more sitting down on it.

Several years passed before she came to be on friendly terms with the neighbours. For Harbans, it happened sooner. The men approached him early on, running an admiring palm along the smooth, clean curves of his new Chevrolet. With Harbans gone, no one padded up in sneakers along the laid-stone path that bifurcated the balanced halves of the front lawn. When Bikram stepped outside, to water or plant bulbs or herbs, the neighbours made their presence known by a darkened triangle of curtain pushed back, where the shape of a face appeared, unmoving. There could be as many as five or six such triangles hiding dark moon faces peering through freshly cleaned glass.

Ravi's appearance changed all this. His bursting energy couldn't be contained by the low brick wall guarding the garden from the sidewalk, and his body soon found itself in neighbours' gardens or playing in the backs of their trucks. On occasion, he was brought home, lost, confused, after wandering into a house thinking it was his own, and at such times the neighbours stopped and briefly chatted and asked Bikram how the rose bushes were doing this year or whether she too was having trouble with gophers. This was how she learned of the new freeway, and all the new houses that were planned for the hills, on ground everyone knew to be unstable and liable to sliding.

Two years of drought, and deer started appearing in the street late at night. Harbans would come home telling of one he almost collided with while exiting the new freeway. Bikram spied them in the mottled, predawn hours, for she remained after all these years an early riser. She no longer had cows to milk or chickens to feed, but the childhood habit stayed.

The first one looked to her like an outline from one of her dreams. The last thing she expected in California, in this modern world, was to see an animal. Weren't people and animals kept apart in the civilized West? She guessed the deer didn't know this, and when dawn silhouetted the backs of houses now visible through the kitchen window, she saw that her roses were gone. Just the flowers, the deer had left the stems.

Bikram inspected the neatly cut stalks and the hoof prints in the soil, slight scars, indistinct chevrons, then she covered the tracks with her own hands, smudging the earth until all that was left were lines marking the passage of her fingers. In the kitchen, she washed her hands, scrubbing her fingernails, and along her forearms. Some days later, a rifle shot rang out, then another, and in the days that followed, several more. Twice, on one of her afternoon walks, she found deer carcasses, no longer shadows or dream shapes, now lying on the crisp, yellow hillside. The mouths gaped open, the bodies swollen and ugly, expanding in the heat. The smell left her unaffected and she approached without fear or revulsion. The gums of the deer were a colony of flies and the hide already filled with holes from where it had been eaten away. An eye bulged yellow and pus leaked from the socket.

She sat with Ravi beside her on the single step that led from the hallway to the living room. The room was furnished with a sofa and a love seat, a Persian rug and a colour RCA television, and on the wall was a wide-view photograph of the Golden Temple. She asked Ravi if he wanted to know the true story of how she had begun to sing, and he said sure, but to be quick, as *Lost in Space* was about to come on and it was his favourite show.

'This is how it happened,' she said, the first time she had ever made so definitive a claim about anything, even though she herself wasn't sure if this was how it happened. How did anything happen? she asked herself. Outside the day was cool, a bright orange scarf of clouds hid the sun. Her memories had merged with songs and the different versions she had told, versions she knew to be false, but falseness seemed appropriate, for how else except through fiction could you recreate a world that had been destroyed?

'It was dawn, no, before dawn. One morning dawn broke early. That's it. Before it should have, and that was how it all started. It broke on the west side of the village, the side where I'd take the buffalo down to the creek for her afternoon drink and where the Mantos had a house. Mrs Manto would call me in as I walked by and hand me a glass of lassi if it was hot. It always tasted so sweet and freshening. There's nothing like it today, you can't make real lassi from milk you buy at Fry's.'

In the mornings she listened to the birds and the frogs, to the scuffling of cows and the three goats, and to the soft squawks of chickens. Her favourite task was to search for freshly laid eggs and carry them back triumphant. That morning she pattered across the mud courtyard and heard the chickens protesting already against the day's heat. The air clung to her skin and she walked to the well to douse her flaming skin. The dome covering it reminded her of the ruined temple, an ancient one that stood in a far corner of the sugarcane fields, engulfed by creepers and home to monkeys and snakes and all sorts of devilish animals.

Water splashed from the bucket as she pulled it up and in small handfuls, she chased it at her skin as the warm breeze cooled her face. Only then did she see it. Or had she sensed it first, listening to the distant scuffles in the animal pen, in a dog's bark, in the faint smell of burning thatch? There, across the western sky, was the false dawn, spilling all over the wrong side of the world. On the horizon stood the bloodied outline of the temple, and from the fields, red fingers spidered into the engulfing bowl of night. Not far from her, houses were already on fire. She could smell it in the air.

They fled with nothing. They took their clothes, some bags of flour, and her mother carried a bag of gold jewellery close to her chest. Only later, when they joined the vast caravan, that artery pumping people across new borders, did they learn of how the world had been split in two, India and Pakistan, and there were no tunes that might link them in song.

'I began to sing on the road. Every day I sang to cheer up my mother and father. They lost many friends, so did I. As we crossed the new border I was singing, and my voice got stuck at the border and because of that I always sing. If I had been chattering, I would always be chattering, and if I was silent, I would never have said another word. What we did at that border, that is how our lives continued, and what we didn't do, we could never do again.'

It was time for Ravi's show, and before she could shoo him away, he was gone and working the controls of the television. Bikram began to hum. It was an old tune from a movie she remembered watching as a young woman. 'Mera joota hai Japani'. My shoes are Japanese.

Children's Games

THE ORPHANAGE, BUILT ON THE OUTSKIRTS OF A RAJ-ERA HILL station, had originally served as a sanatorium for injured soldiers who had survived the 1857 revolt. Some years before the end of the century it was converted into a private school for children of officials of the Raj. Finally, a Presbyterian minister from New Hampshire bought the failing school and transformed it in the early decades of the twentieth century into an orphanage and dayschool primarily for Anglo-Indian children. My own arrival, like most, was unheralded, and I retained few memories of those first days, another lost child among so many lost children.

The architecture was imported: a decayed Gothic hovering in the roofs and windows giving little inkling of utility or purpose. The buildings were arrayed along a ridge and not far from the school, the roads afforded lush views of the surrounding valleys. The mouldering brown or dull orange of the stone took on the colours, in the late afternoon and twilight, of the rougher, darker ground, as though the architecture, in the morning and daylight, was an illusion that fractured, giving itself up with the dying sun as it returned to the singular entropy of the dirt's crushed brown surface. Reverend Healdstone served as principal and pastor. He was a tall man with thick arms and in the afternoons I would hear the clack of an axe as he chopped wood, the sharp, dying rustle of branches as he scythed through encroaching brush. In the days of the hill station, an artificial lake had been dug on the far outskirts. It lived on as a swamp, filled in mostly, home to water snakes and insects of every variety, an ugly, unstable ground few dared approach, smelling of refuse and excrement, slushing underfoot if trudged across.

In the centre of the courtyard a massive stone pillar lay on its side. Neither base nor top had survived and much of the decoration that had once been carved on it had been lost or chipped away by soldiers or children. The inscription remained visible in areas and arrayed over its crumbling surface were several symbols whose menace invited attempts at interpretation: two dots became a face, a line became a knife, a circle was for us a decapitated head. There was a beauty to the decayed surface of the pillar, especially at certain hours, when the etched relief, made splendid in the slanting rays of the sun, took on the proportions of a grand history: now the dots were stars shooting through the sky, the line became a door leading to the hall of a great and glittering palace.

The teachers claimed it was erected by the great Emperor Ashoka, one of his famous pillars cut in the third century BC, inscribed with his laws and spread all across the land untold eons ago. Vines struggled up its sides and enclosed the soft grey stone under a mossy sleep while the climate nibbled at it through a slow mastication by the elements. I once discovered a history of architecture in the school library which contained a print of the pillar. In the drawing the pillar appeared much larger and no houses surrounded it yet. A man dressed in a dhoti stood idly by for scale and behind him trees arched to fill the landscape. The author claimed that though some had counted this among Ashoka's pillars, he was certain it was not. The inscriptions dated from several centuries later. It was perhaps an imitation, though a good one, yet clearly not the real thing.

When I showed Mr Babcock, the English and Latin teacher, the print of the Ashokan pillar and the author's claim that it was a forgery, he laughed. He shook his head from side to side, showing all his teeth, and snatched the book away, looking at it first upside down then right way up, telling me it didn't matter if it was a fake or not. He tossed the book dismissively onto his desk, sending up a cloud of dust. Everything in this godforsaken country, he said, was a fake! Even I was a forgery!

Mr Babcock was a short, balding man and in the evenings, when I found him in his room or sitting on the verandah, he would be clutching a glass of beer or gin. He never showed his drunkenness. That was the single rule of the orphanage, its last redoubt against collapse: that as long as moral deterioration remained hidden, there lived a possibility of redemption. But few of the teachers were good at dissembling their carelessness and classes were odd affairs where a teacher would stand at the front and talk, often dictating, seldom checking work for accuracy, simply ensuring we had filled pages and not made too much noise.

Such freedom was a burdensome, agoraphobic freedom. We could do almost anything, but in a world bounded by the atrophied wills of our keepers, we found ourselves unmoored and without purpose. We were afraid to leave the grounds and we created tales of all the horrors awaiting us in the old lake, along the ridge, in the houses in the valley, the dark recesses of the town's shops. Djinns mocked us from every gate and window. We looked to each other for structure and for boundaries to our actions and worlds and what felt like a natural hierarchy developed, or perhaps showed itself, freed of the imposed hierarchies of parents and teachers.

Those at the top were the orphans. We owned the grounds and the dayschoolers could never better our knowledge and sense of freedom among the buildings and fields. Among us orphans there were those who had been left by parents and those who had lived here since they could remember, who knew nothing or little of their past. These latter formed the apex of our hierarchy, its College of Bishops, its Senate, and here skin colour, age and strength gave rise to our leaders. Those with the lightest skin, a skin almost European in tint, always occupied the highest rungs. My own skin was clearly brown, a light shade, and so though near the top (because I had no memories of any place other than the orphanage) I never found myself at the highest point of our invented mountain of souls.

The day Howard found a monkey's skull reshaped our vision of him and of ourselves, it shifted the crustal plates of our small world at the orphanage. Howard was a tall, lanky boy who looked like he should already be wearing pants. Most years, he was at the top of our self-created hierarchy and swaggered about, amiable but fierce in his authority, and we accepted his position without thought or protest, as though it was another game whose rules we had all agreed upon years ago. The skull was a brilliant white, the colour of a newly white-washed wall with the paint still infecting the air around it with its burying odour. The teeth in the maxilla were intact, though the lower jaw was missing. The canines were a fabulous vision of our carnivorous selves and we mimicked them when he showed us this strange prize of a sortie out to the old lake. I thought of him stamping about in those noxious, forbidden tracts that held so much terror for us all. It was a brave act and gave his find the aura of an object carried back from a forbidden expedition.

None of us had seen a monkey's skull before and when he claimed it was the skull of one of our ancestors, a proto-human, Krishnanthropus he labelled it, we all believed him. 'One of *your* ancestors,' he insisted in the sing-song voice of childhood certainty, 'not mine. I don't come from anything so low.' Howard said that *anthropology*, for this is what he termed what he was doing—a new word for all of us—was a hit and miss thing: you might be lucky to find a tooth, let alone a skull with its jaw. We applauded him and danced around him, making wild monkey noises, until Mr Babcock, driven from his afternoon lethargy by our exuberance, demanded to know what all the ruckus was after. He was drunk and we all knew it and we laughed at him, right in his face, an incredible show of defiance, one we had never allowed ourselves before, and it pulled us all, I am sure, to the edges of our own possible worlds. Howard was the first to laugh, mimicking perfectly Mr Babcock's swaying gait, his demand to know what was happening, his confusion, his annoyance at being disturbed. We all quickly followed, ourselves drunk on the sudden liberty of Howard's capering free, while Mr Babcock stood within our threatening circle, cheeks reddening, saying nothing, until that final retreat in which he walked drunkenly across the dusty courtyard, back to his rooms on the far side of the complex of buildings.

We were terrified for a night and day after waiting for the coming punishment, yet none admitted his fear. We issued empty threats, mocking Babcock and Healdstone—bravado all the way round, for every one of us awaited the coming punishment with unspoken terror. The night and day and the following night and day passed without reaction and only on the third day did we suspect they would not punish us. At first we celebrated this fact as our victory with Arjun dancing like a monkey and Howard claiming that now we were in control. But as the withholding of the punishment continued, carrying over from three days to a week and then two weeks, we felt a growing oppression, waiting there for us. In Healdstone's every gesture during morning assembly we expected his violent reaction, and when every gesture admitted only his daily recalcitrance and disregard, our fear only enlarged. We felt it like a pressure growing, sitting over us, the certainty of a coming doom in this slow suffocation through our haphazard reprieve.

Neither teachers nor servants knew of Krishnanthropus. Howard kept his find well hidden. 'If they get it,' he said, 'they'll take all the credit. I've written letters to scientists in Europe and America and even Africa. I'm sure someone will come soon.' The writing of letters was to us an incredible endeavour, almost Herculean, because it pushed us out into the world, the far wide world, and we believed we were not a part of it, that we lived on the fringes of its farthest periphery. What splendid arrogance on the side of Howard, an arrogance that awed us all.

He kept the skull secured in a place none could find, though twice we organized expeditions to search for it. He brought it out at night, displayed it on an unstable wooden table at the back of an abandoned room in what was once a prison. The skull would sit alone and we were required, if we wanted to view it, to bring a present or offering or garland. We carried sweets and flowers and comic books and fruit and toys and piled them up, Howard standing behind the table all the while, following us with his eyes. He said nothing as the procession of children pushed inside. Behind him, in niches in the wall, two candles burned and bathed us in their vacillating glow. After presenting our gifts we knelt, even Howard, and lowered our heads in obeisance to this strange god from whom we were all, or all except Howard, created. Thus the ceremony ended always in eerie silence. Nothing was ever said and the meeting was always brief. The next day we would see Howard walking casually with the comic book one of us had left fluttering in his hand, nibbling on the sweet some child had offered, quite openly and without comment, and we accepted it as his privilege: he was not descended from the skull, we were; he was its discoverer, the discoverer of our origins, and this placed a distance between him and the rest of us, only increasing our restrained admiration and fear.

Up to then, I had been the boy everyone knew could answer any question; it was me the others came to if they needed help with their French or Latin or geography or history. Howard was little more than an athlete and a poor student. But finding the skull and naming it, giving it a history, his letters to scientists, now made him preeminent amongst us, not only in physical activities but in everything. If anyone had a question, they turned to him. No matter if he didn't know, he would make the answer up or say he would tell them later. If he delayed answering, he often came secretly to consult me and I could not help but tell him. We were all a little in love with him, with his white skin and brown hair that in the sunlight shone almost red or blond. He was seldom angry, even when he lost a fight to a boy he knew was weaker than himself. We believed this was magnanimity, a largeness of his person, we believed he had a right to beat up any boy he chose. It was taken for granted, something in the air we breathed; we could see how the teachers treated him. They never scolded him, even when he scored poorly on exams. If another student failed he might be sent to wash the walls of the kitchen, to give him time to think over poor study habits or lack of diligence, but when Howard failed, and he failed often, he was simply given a lecture, 'This is not good enough, is it? Not your usual, is it? Well, better next time, eh.' And that was all, as though some divine dispensation was invoked over his every failure; and his successes were transformed into the equivalents of great military victories: a mediocre essay by Howard would be read as an example of brilliance, toward which we should all strive (even though in all likelihood I had written the essay and had deliberately dumbed it down).

One day Howard received a reply from one of the scientists. None of us recognized the name but the envelope, which he showed us, presented a crown on its reverse side, the Royal Academy of something or other, and we were all impressed and a little terrified at its meaning. Not only had Howard dared to send a message out into the world, a bottle from our island of shipwrecked isolation, but he had received a reply. A ship's sail cut across our horizon and we were all afraid of its imminent arrival, of the nearing end of our lost condition. He read it that night at a special meeting called in the prison. The skull rested in its usual spot, sitting on large, green leaves and surrounded by a mass of offerings almost hiding it from view. Up to now, no one had ever spoken at these meetings. There was a bond of silence born both out of a reverence and awe for the skull and a fear of being discovered, and even Howard appeared reluctant to break this tradition, as though words might shatter what tenuous web had been strung between us these past several weeks.

Arjun sat beside me, fidgeting and afraid. He was my closest friend among the boys and I knew he never enjoyed these meetings. He was afraid of the dark and of cramped places and was always the last to enter and the first to leave.

It was a surprise to me that he could ever tolerate the library, but he would often scurry in, searching for some particular volume, and take it with him to read outside in the dusty courtyard. Howard's silence lengthened. I could feel his nervousness growing and it infected me with a restlessness and a fear different from his. The candles stood behind him and what little light shone on his face was reflected light and so it was more a shadow with the vague inscription of eyes and mouth and nose, like a copperplate with an etched design.

In the letter the scientist thanked Howard for his note. His name was Dr Wilson, a professor of dentistry. He said the skull described sounded more like a modern chimpanzee's or baboon's than any human ancestor's, though if Howard wished, he could certainly send along a photograph. He would ask friends who knew about these things, charm-stones and bones. Had Howard read much about the Egyptians? There was a people, was there not, eh? The letter ended with a note saying that the world needed more such bully observant and intelligent boys like Howard, and when he grew up he should send along another letter. Maybe there'd be a spot in the school of dentistry.

I could not see Howard's expression when he finished reading but I could guess from his faltering voice a growing and stiffening anger that held his body tight in the dim light of the old prison. Finally he bent forward and in that single bending forward was contained his defeat. He took the letter and tore it in two and then he tore these pieces again and again until only shreds survived. These he let drop through his fingers and to the floor and onto the table, some landing among the gifts piled up for our strange ancestor. We did not bow down. Instead, Howard, in a voice holding back a childish and compressed rage, said simply, 'What can that old fart know? What can anyone know?'

Arjun was shaking. I could feel his arm pressed against mine. It was hot with sweat. I turned to look at him. His eyes were closed and his mouth was shut tight and his body dipped forward and backward with slight undulating motions like a cat drinking milk. He sprang up when Howard said we should go and was out through the door and lost in the night of the buildings and stars and trees and the intimation of a village beyond. The night was cool, a conjuring blackness, and as I stepped briefly into it, the other children around me, I felt the sudden oppressiveness of their bodies surrounding me.

The following day, Howard came to see me. I was hiding in the library. I had found a book on London in the thirties, the London before the war, and I was dreaming of the Lambeth Walk and Knees Up, Mother Brown. I thought of myself travelling there, like Vasco da Gama on his voyage to India, slaughtering infidels along the way, being guided by the gods, and finding a land so strange, so different, a whole other world. It seemed like that to me, these creatures who did the Lambeth Walk, who drank pints and played billiards and darts, and offered as real a world to conquer as did the India of da Gama's time. To me, England, France, the United States were all constituents of a single continent whose features I could not easily define, but within which

Shakespeare lived alongside Hitler, The Beatles sang and Mozart composed, where George Washington daily crossed the Potomac and Coca-Cola was drunk in draft pints.

Howard said to me, 'Something's got to happen.' He was wearing a white shirt and black shorts and suspenders and the white of his legs and arms was stark and unmitigated in the dimness of the library as though he was a being visiting me from another dimension, from a heaven or a hell. He brought his face close to mine, ignoring what I was reading.

'Happen? What do you mean?'

'We have to do something for Krishna.' He called the skull Krishna now because when he tried to pronounce the whole name, he got it mixed up or confused. His voice was charged with an excitement I had never heard before in him and his breath tickled my cheek in quick, easy puffs. 'We have to get the chaps together and do something. They're already losing interest. You saw it last night. Some didn't want to be there. They didn't care.'

I thought he was accusing me directly, because I had already lost interest. I didn't know what the fuss was about anymore, and though the secretiveness of the meetings had originally excited me, it was clear Howard had no idea what to do with them or how to use them. He simply stood there and took the gifts as though that was sufficient. I wanted to tell him we all worshipped him, we all waited for a word from him; we would do anything, but he had to tell us, to lead us.

'It's boring,' I said.

'But this is your ancestor. That's what you come from. Don't you understand?'

I knew I didn't come from that and I thought of telling this to Howard, but demanded instead, 'But where do *you* come from?'

'Not that.' His tone was dismissive and this angered me. 'Only you come from that,' he carried on. 'Only you blackies.'

'You're not bloody different.'

'But I don't come from that. I can't. I found it. I come from some European ape.'

'My mother was French,' I said, unsure why.

'Liar!'

'Yes, she was!'

Howard burst out, 'She was one of those whores in town! Haven't you seen them? The ones with the—'

Before he could finish, I raised a fist and punched him in the stomach. He fell back, mostly from surprise, into a wall of books. He was up in a moment and on top of me, scrambling his fists and attacking me with fury. I fought back as best I could but I was no match for him and soon my kicks and thrusts were completely smothered. He took my head in his hands and struck it against the tiled floor.

'She was a fucking whore! A fucking whore! They were all fucking whores! Don't you get it? Don't you know why we're here?'

I screamed and Howard knocked my head harder against the tiles. Through the sudden pain, I heard footsteps running and a voice, and I could see Mr Babcock's feet and legs standing close by.

He said, 'Howard,' his voice thin and weak. It was closer to a question than an injunction. Then again, 'Howard? Let Vijay go?' Howard raised and dropped my head once more and Babcock repeated, 'Howard, will you let the little chap go now?'

Howard's breath was hard and fast in my ears.

He eventually stopped, though more from exhaustion than from Babcock's pathetic entreaties. Babcock crouched beside me. I could smell tobacco and alcohol on his breath and he looked weakly at my face as though I was both there and not there, as though to him I existed in two possible states and he had not yet decided which of those two was real. He fell back a moment, losing his balance, and then he righted himself again. Finally, he seemed to decide. 'Vijay?' he said in a voice expressing surprise and recognition. 'Why did you make Howard do that?'

I began to cry. I looked down at the tiles. There was a smear of blood there and I raised a hand to my head and felt my wet hair. I brought the fingers to my face. They were red and I showed this to Mr Babcock as though it was an explanation for everything, and if not an explanation, then at least an expiation, a confession of my guilt and complicity. Howard stood silently behind Mr Babcock. He did not look at me but instead looked away and out through the door, though from his angle he could see only a few feet down along the hall. Perhaps he was expecting someone else, perhaps this had all been strangely planned. Mr Babcock studied my hand and shook his head. 'You're cut up,' he said and I was surprised because I thought he must be saying something more than the plainly obvious but that I was too dumb to comprehend it.

'Before I take you to the nurse, will you say sorry to Howard.'

The look I gave him must have shaken him because he did not repeat the request, instead he told me brusquely to stand and walk with him. To Howard he said, 'You go clean yourself up, young chap.' Howard nodded but did not move, waiting for us to leave before he followed us out of the library.

I walked with Babcock's wavering hand on my shoulder, Howard's steps shadowing mine. I could feel the blood dripping along my face, mingling with tears. I was furious and hated Howard and hated Babcock and hated myself for not fighting, for following Howard for as long as I had. I was ashamed and every step I took battled with that shame, held it up, magnified it, toppled it, recreated it.

That night I slept in the infirmary and in the evening I watched as several boys, fewer than usual, crept from the dormitory and out across the courtyard to the prison. Arjun was among them. They looked like ghosts floating over the ground, gliding in and out of light and dark, the faint sound of their steps disappearing into the swallowing blackness.

The first command Howard delivered from the skull of the Krishnanthropus was that all children must play only those games Howard decided upon. This was not a large demand as Howard already controlled most games played in the courtyard and around the ancient stone pillar. If he wanted to play king of the hill, that's what we played, and if he wanted to play cricket, that's also what we played, and for several days there was no outward change from the regular round of games between or after classes. The Krishnanthropus had simply codified a part of the structure of our lives and many of us continued to play as we wanted to, ignoring Howard completely, asking him to join or not join as we wished, and I, soon after that first pronouncement, forgot it until the afternoon I was sitting in the shade of a tamarind tree playing chess with Arjun. Arjun was winning and we were approaching the game's end when Howard walked up, shifting from foot to foot as he stood there in the bright sunlight.

Howard didn't look at me. Since the day in the library he had avoided talking to me or finding himself being left alone with me, and now his face conceded my presence only through the stiffness and withdrawal of his expression. In his hand he held the branch of a tree with two tapered green leaves still attached. Earlier I had seen him playing some game of war, acting the general in command.

When he spoke, he looked directly at Arjun. 'You can't play that anymore. It's not allowed.' He sputtered this quickly, almost breathlessly.

Arjun looked first at Howard and then toward me and then back to Howard.

'But—' Arjun protested.

'That's what it said, remember? You agreed. I was to decide.'

I broke in, 'You can't tell us not to play.'

Howard ignored me. 'Are you coming?' he demanded of Arjun.

'But the game's almost over,' Arjun offered. 'I'm winning.'

'It's a forbidden game now.' Howard spoke with a strained authority that didn't match his voice, making him sound foolish, and I mimicked his anxious command.

'It's a forbidden game now.'

Arjun looked back at me but now his eyes displayed clear unease. He moved his head slowly back and forth along a compressed arc. Howard raised the stick by an inch and Arjun's eyes flashed away from mine and across to Howard's hand.

'Don't listen to that monkey,' Howard said. His hand was shaking.

'It's a forbidden game now,' I repeated, raising the pitch of my voice to make the command sound even more comical.

Howard turned to look at me. 'We'll get you,' he said. There was a pathetic violence in his voice. Even on the day in the library I had not detected this tone. He turned back to Arjun. 'Come on,' he said. Arjun stood quickly, not looking at me or the chessboard. Within a few moves he would have won, but now his figure angled away from me with Howard behind him. The kids beyond still played war and I watched Arjun walk away from me and felt a hot, suffocating shame spread up along my cheeks until it reached my eyes and I could feel it pressing at my eyelids. I called out in a mocking voice, 'Forbidden game, forbidden game,' but neither turned and soon I could see Arjun joining in the game of war, holding high a quickly fashioned weapon, and shrieking as he ran in a pack with his fellow combatants.

From that time on, most of the boys ignored me. I had few close friends among the other children except Arjun and we knew each other the way kids know each other, who play together and sleep together, with a friendship resting at the edges of our common interests: checkers, chess, books of travel, distant lands and times. There was no real closeness between us and I was not wholly surprised when Arjun turned his back on me as easily as the others. Now when one of the kids spoke to me, it was a brief comment or a sentence, only said when we found ourselves alone together. At night, Arjun slipped notes to me, telling me of the latest commands of Howard and the Krishnanthropus. The notes were brief and cryptic, speaking of another world coalescing at the edges of my own. This was how I learned the Krishnanthropus had ordered no one was to talk or play with me. I was both relieved and disturbed and told myself the skull was stupid and the games and orders that came from it childish. My lonely hours in the library or in the long dormitory now lengthened and when boys would come across me or be startled by my form entering a room, hiding at a desk, playing alone in the courtyard or among the trees, they looked at me with pitying scorn. I hated them for this stare because it was the gaze I wanted to give back to them.

The notes Arjun left for me under my pillow or in the pages of a book I was reading contained brief versions of Howard's edicts. These were short, impenetrable messages, messages from an unknown god, except we all knew who the god was: Howard. This was now his world, and this was how he would rule it: 'K says no more chess', 'Prison tonight. Extra gifts', 'Tell all no skull', 'Talk brings pain', 'Pillar is history says K', 'Play only in yard', 'K the old one', 'Avoid the pillar'. The day after this last note, there were no children to be found on the pillar. It had existed as the centre of our activities for so long that its abandonment shocked me. Howard's power and hold over the children, particularly those who lived inside the school, had clearly grown. When one of the day students approached the pillar during the mid-morning break, I watched Arjun run up to him and violently thrust him away. There were the beginnings of a fight between the two but several boys rallied behind Arjun and soon the one who had approached the pillar stalked off, waving a hand dismissively in the air.

I found Arjun alone in the toilet that same day. He looked at me sheepishly when I spoke to him.

'I don't know anything anymore,' he said, taking his eyes from mine and looking beyond me to the door. 'I think Howard pays the servants. How else does he stop them from talking?'

'But why can't you play on the pillar?'

'The old one says the pillar is a symbol of a false god.'

'But it's one of Ashoka's—'

'The old one says that all history must be destroyed because it's false. He was here before history. He wants to come back. To start history again.'

'The old one?'

'He speaks through Krishna.'

'Bugger the old one,' I said violently and loudly.

Arjun gave me a look of alarm and then cast his eyes down to the floor. 'I don't know who's right.'

'Not Howard.'

'But Howard speaks with it. He does. He wants to start everything over, to begin the world again. He says we're the only ones who can, without parents, without history. That's what he says.' Arjun's voice was almost pleading and he seemed very changed from the Arjun I had known.

'I don't care,' I said. 'He's a bastard.'

Arjun shook his head and when I demanded more, he said nothing. He pressed his lips tightly together and refused to look at me until finally he said, 'The old one says you're part of the false world. The false world will pass.' Then he walked out, not looking back at me. When he was gone I looked around at the stark, brown walls with a single glassless window facing the back wall of the compound. A kid stood staring at me from that wall. I recognized him as one of the younger dayschoolers who shadowed Howard's every step.

That night Arjun returned to the bed next to mine and hid his face in his hands, moving stiffly in the dim light cast by candles burning at the far end of the room. He pulled the blanket up with tense motions of his limbs and later whimpered quietly as though troubled by nightmares. When I whispered his name, he stopped making any sound. I lay awake for an hour, watching the slow progress of his breath as it raised and lowered the sheet over his thin frame. In the morning I saw the bruises on his face. He must have seen the look of surprise on my face because he turned immediately away and pulled on his clothes without comment. No one spoke to anyone and we all shuffled out of the dormitory to breakfast in a gaping silence.

All day the children continued like this, hardly speaking to one another, and when they did, it was a hushed sentence, a whisper pressed to an ear. After lunch, when we were allowed out to play, some gathered around the pillar, sitting on it, leaning against it. No one had gathered here for days. I watched them from a window in the library. I was reading a book written by a geologist in the middle of the previous century. It was a journal of his travels around India, and contained information not only about the geology but about bird and animal life, about the landscapes and the people he encountered. In Oudh he discovered several tales of wolf-boys, children stolen from their families at birth by wolves and reared in feral packs. When they were found and captured, they never assimilated back into society: they would eat only raw meat, they tore to shreds any clothes they were given, ran around on all fours, and never talked, only howled or whimpered, pining for a lost freedom. I was affected by the description of the silence of the boys; I began to see myself like them, lost to the society of the orphanage children. I had been thrown out of its orbit, thrown into a state of feral silence.

Later I approached the pillar in the cool early evening. I didn't care if anyone saw me. The pillar was covered with the initials of every student, newly inscribed. This is how they had spent the afternoon when they had gathered on it in a pack. Every boy's initials were there, or all but mine. I felt a curious vertigo on seeing new letters scratched into the old stone, a sickening unease, and later when I found Arjun alone I stopped him with a hand and demanded to know what was going on.

'That's my stone!' I shouted at him, hitting him in the chest with a fist. 'It's mine! You can't do anything to it. I'll tell.'

Arjun looked at me and said nothing. Finally he pulled away and ran from me and I began to cry. I don't know why I cried except that I felt a sudden and overwhelming isolation. I hated them, every last one.

That night the boys went to bed as usual. It was the cricket instructor, Mr Ellis's turn to walk the dorm. He stamped across the floorboards noisily, inspecting every bunk, shaking this child's foot or peering closely at another's face. He was a harsh, recalcitrant man who demanded roughly from each one of us whether we were asleep and we were all required to answer in bright voices that yes sir, we were most definitely asleep. When he was gone, I tried to stay awake because I knew something would happen that night. But within minutes I was lost and when I woke I looked across to Arjun's bed and found it empty. The bed on the other side of me was empty also. I sat up quickly, letting the sheet slide down my body. All the other beds were abandoned and I was left entirely alone. The room was cool and I felt the chilly night air playing over my body.

A window framed the dark courtyard and the black shape of the pillar. Only a thin moon shone and no lights showed in any windows. I could see almost nothing. The pillar looked like a darkening of the surrounding blackness, as though in this single spot night had curdled in the stiffening summer heat. The sounds of insects filled the air with their insistent scraping. A minute passed before I made out the shapes of the children. They stood about the pillar and on it, thickening it, smothering it, engulfing it with their bodies, giving it a second skin with the gift of their own backs. I felt a sickening weakness come over me and for some seconds stood paralyzed, watching. They were on my pillar. I walked barefoot toward the door with empty beds on either side of me, holding my hands out to protect myself against any objects obstructing my path.

The children were like locusts swarmed over the pillar and the motion of their bodies made the pillar appear to move and writhe, bucking and squirming like a massive pupa of a great insect beast waiting to be born. The sound of metal scraping against stone rose and fell above the noise of disinterested insects. No one looked at me as I walked toward the pillar. The ground shimmered in the thin film of moonlight, a membrane that hid below its translucent surface a buried fire, golden embers still glowing after some ancient eruption. Every boy was on the pillar now, or standing by it, or on his knees at its side. In their hands they held knives or forks with which they scraped against the surface of the pillar. I saw Howard on top of it, kneeling among the other children, his arms working feverishly, battering at the stone, gouging at it with a knife in each hand. He would look up every few moments to goad the others on. 'Come on, come on,' he demanded. Just that. 'Come on, come on,' ever repeated. There was a haze of dust visible around the boys' bodies that made them appear unreal and phantom-like. The longer I stared, the more ethereal and otherworldly they looked. I walked as though approaching an apparition. I could hear their breaths, stark and insistent, and years later I would imagine it as an orgy nearing its climax. I found Arjun leaning against the pillar, working at one side of it. I pushed his shoulder violently and he turned and looked at me in shock. His face was white with dust. I wanted to shout at him but found myself unable to express any words. For some seconds he showed no recognition and then his face transformed into something angry and ugly and he spat at my leg and turned quickly away and continued his frantic work with heightened fury; his body moved as though he was humping this beast, fucking it, fissuring and raping it, an abysmal initiation into the manhood of destruction, causing great white clouds of dust to rise and coalesce in the filmy light. Their voices were the pants of dogs, their tongues pushed out, pulled in, their thin arms strained. They looked ridiculous and terrifying. I could taste the harsh chalk of the dust. I could feel it on my skin, between my fingers, clogging my throat. I wanted to stop them, to scream at them, but could only stand and stare, paralyzed, in mute testimony, knowing that my anger lay as much in my exclusion from their ranks as at their actions.

I watched this scene for minutes as their bodies heaved up and down, in and out, tossed on some wave, as though they had caught a great fish and were riding its back, sticking their harpoons in, one after the other, trying to push into the kill, trying to cut its life off, but the fish wouldn't die, it kept them on, it kept the chase on, racing through more and distant waters, pulling them along, raising them up, throwing them down, drowning them, rescuing them; they were losing home and ship, all hope of land, all hope of ever pulling in the flesh of this beast; their charts were gone, their instruments lost, the sky a black cave offering no stars for guidance, knowledge of the winds eradicated; their voices worked in snarling, urgent breaths and the knives and forks battled at the sides, trying to force any and all capitulation. But the fish pulled them along, out out out to the farthest reaches of the oceans where even the islands believed themselves to be whole worlds unto themselves, alone and without companion.